TRUE ASH

TRUE ASH

ELIZABETH J. COLEN
& CAROL GUESS

Black
Lawrence
Press

Black
Lawrence
Press

www.blacklawrence.com

Executive Editor: Diane Goettel
Book and Cover Design: Amy Freels
Cover Art: "Meadowlands No. 9" by Corinne Botz

Copyright © Elizabeth J. Colen and Carol Guess 2018
ISBN: 978-1-62557-702-3

Published 2018 by Black Lawrence Press.
Printed in the United States.

CONTENTS

TRUE ASH

If trees could talk, you said. If they could tell us what they saw.

But if you didn't want to talk about it, why would a tree?

We walked in the arboretum as if nothing had happened. Past Japanese Maples, Witch Hazels, Legumes. Through Pinetum and across the stone footbridge. The math of it, was what you said.

We stopped to eat among Hollies and Hawthorns. When you sliced an apple, the red cored curl made me want to ask questions. The thing that had happened was unlikely to happen again, but you needed to be sure, so you carried a knife. You wanted me to carry one, too, but I was clumsy and sometimes fell. Even in the arboretum I liked to wear heels, the kind most women wear at night. It felt safer to wear heels during the day. At night I wore flats, shoes that could run.

When we got back to your apartment, I always cleaned the bottom of my heels with a paper towel. I did this sitting on the floor in my skirt, and sometimes you watched, lifting my hem. After a while I stopped wearing anything underneath my skirt and our walks got shorter.

There was nothing unusual about them, you said.

Who? I asked. We were eating dinner at your place.

The couple, you said. In the arboretum. The couple I saw in True Ashes that day.

I thought you said it happened in Hollies.

God no, you said. Nothing like that.

I sprinkled salt on my salad. Sometimes I ate salty things and sometimes sweet, but never at once. You claimed you couldn't tell salt and sugar apart. But you said that about a lot of things.

I thought about all the couples I'd seen walking in the arboretum. How the woman sometimes bent into the man as if she couldn't walk on her own. How the man explained the names of trees while she extended her branches.

We're not like that, you said.

But what did you mean?

I wanted to ask what it was that you'd seen. I'd avoided the news for a week after that. You saw it first, from the outside, a stranger. On the cusp of True Ashes, and who knew what they saw.

Maybe trees bend toward us on purpose.

Sunlight, you said. The science of roots.

But maybe it's more. Maybe they feel things.

Would you stop eating plants if you knew what they felt?

I didn't answer, just rubbed my ring across my wrist.

You lifted my hem. Bunched my skirt around my waist and straddled me. My shoes and hands were dirty, but you wanted my mouth, so it didn't matter.

The couple, I asked. What was she wearing?

Did I mention a woman?

I assumed they were straight.

You smirked.

So it was two men. Or two women? Who else could it be, walking in pairs?

♦

The next morning you went to work and I worked from your apartment. It was part of our agreement to trade. Sometimes your upstairs neighbor played music, pot smoke drifting down through the vents.

At noon I walked to the corner store for a sandwich. While I was browsing I noticed a pack of bubblegum cigarettes. I hadn't seen that kind of candy in years. Something about advertising smoking to children.

Can I have these for half? I asked.

The clerk looked at the date on the faded pink wrapper.

Just take them. We don't even carry those here.

I put the pack in my pocket. Bought coffee and a loaf of bread. Walked from the store to the arboretum. Scattered bread, waited for birds.

They swooped down from the sky to land at my feet.

If you would wait. If you would stand very still.

When you came home that night you asked if I'd gone there.

Why do you ask?

Because of the dirt.

It was true. I'd tracked dirt through the kitchen. In the movies you liked, girls licked the floor clean.

I scrubbed with a towel while you uncorked a bottle. Then you poured two glasses and we sat on the couch.

◆

In the morning you were gone again. I couldn't remember the kiss, if there had been one, how long, mouths open or closed. All I was left with was the dream, but no one wants to hear about that. Everything the color raw umber, everything shaded and drawn. I went looking again.

I liked that the woods had a name here. Arboretum. Sometimes I got glossolalic about it. Sometimes it turned into other things. Our bore eat them. Arrr burr, arrr boar. Eee tomb. A tomb.

What had you seen? I texted you all day. And followed couples. Took pictures while their backs were turned. Them? I texted, with photo. Them? To the pictures you offered no response. Only: stop that. You'll get yourself in trouble. So I stopped that. Was someone taking pictures, I asked. No. Was someone hurt. No. Was there blood. Absolutely not. Well what was it. I took a picture of the sky and you told me: closer. And then the day was filled with meetings, you with your people, me with the trees. Near noon I looked at my watch to see if I could be hungry. The stippled light made my wrist look bark-like just for a second. Then a crow chattered and I was me again.

Did you work today, you asked when you got home. I told you I tried to, but you didn't know what that meant. You took off your shoes and all I could think was that your feet were ugly, but that I liked all of the ugly in you. At ten, like always, you held my wrists behind me and pushed me up against the stove. I liked my hands on you, but you liked them behind me. No, you told me when I tried to get free. That's not how this is going to be. Your face was full of drink and I went stiff until you quit.

What did you see?

What?

What did you see?

But you were out, snoring, sawing zees. I put on the noise machine, turned it to birds and mapped out the park in my head. Everything green, but the ashes were glowing.

♦

I went to see my mother in Auburn and sat so long watching talk shows I couldn't get up from the chair. She was talking about men with red hair again. Why always this I didn't know. And hats. Cloche and fedora, schoolboy and beret. At least it wasn't the shadows. Sometimes she saw people who weren't there. Sometimes my father. Sometimes another one of me. Was I a twin, I started to wonder. I tried to pay attention. Ginger, she said. Ginger? Ginger, their hair. I hit my legs, but they were wooden. I hit them again; they softened a bit. My legs felt filled with water. I felt I could spread out again.

You called to tell me not to come home, that you would be late anyway. I thought it was good to be out in the sun, or, the light like flame on the carpet from the skylight. I let it lead me around the room. I stretched out in it, lifted my face to it. Is it strange, I thought and then texted, that I swear I can feel my hair grow. You never responded. Just two words to say goodnight: sleep well.

♦

What did you see?

What?

What did you see?

Are we back to this again?

Out of the corner of my eye I saw an axe in your hand, but it was just the chain and you led me around, or it was just your two rings catching the light.

Come here, you told me. And I did as you said. I started to touch your face, but you said it tickled. In the lamplight you looked a little green. I couldn't see myself in you.

Close your eyes, you told me. And I was sure I'd never open them again, so I didn't.

Count to ten, you said. But I didn't.

On the bed, you told me. And that wasn't a question. My knees went out from under me. But you changed your mind.

Open your eyes. But they were already open.

On your feet. They felt out of control. I put on my heels.

Out the door. You may as well have collared and leashed me.

I was in front of you all the way, you giving directions. Right at the Hollies, left at the Dogwoods, straight through the copse of Magnolia. They smelled sticky and sweet. Dead blooms blackened underfoot.

Don't turn around, you told me. But I wouldn't have thought of it. Don't speak. I said nothing.

Into the stand of True Ash my heels sank slow as you stopped me. My toes found soil, that damp cold, and began to tunnel down. My legs were striated and hard, hard husk, a cortex, a casing, outer shell. My head felt light and the wind began to move through me. You kissed my shoulder, hand heavy at the back of my neck. You got me down on my knees, but that wasn't low enough. I disappeared in the leaves.

THE APPEASEMENT

Marketing was always late. Sometimes she didn't even show, and the meeting went on without her. If legal didn't show, forget it. But marketing was this gray area, where we all felt like we could do her job. So first she was late, and then no show, and then the cops turned up in the lobby.

I was talking to Felice. Just talking. My wife at home, two kids, the end. Suddenly cops; there went that conversation. I ate lunch at my desk, but no one knew squat.

This was Friday. I spent the weekend at home. Had sex for the first time in how many months. Worked out at the gym, washed the car, mowed the lawn. Took the kids to a movie. Nothing too deep.

On Monday Brianna drove the kids to swim practice, but her power walking buddy canceled, so she was home by 8. I followed her into the bedroom. She was sorting laundry, little piles of clean.

"Wanna grab breakfast?"

"I've got stuff to do."

I thought about asking for a blow job, but figured she'd like that even less than an eggwich. Instead I ate by myself at one of the food trucks. Watched traffic creep past boats on the bay.

When I got to work the lobby was quiet. I caught an elevator right away. Swiped my badge while I texted Felice.

How was yr weekend? ☺

The elevator didn't move.

Swiped my card six, seven times. Got out of the elevator and walked to front desk. It wasn't Herschel. Some guy named Frank.

"I work on 10, but my card won't swipe."

Frank's mouth did something weird.

"I can prove that I work here. Want to call upstairs?"

"You're not going upstairs. I have orders to escort all 10th floor employees out of the building."

"But my stuff," I said. What I meant was Felice.

Frank gestured toward the door. "Let's go."

"It's the cigarettes, isn't it?"

"Exit the building."

"I knew it!" I pounded my fist on his desk.

"You need to leave now or I'm calling security."

"Aren't you security?"

Frank picked up the phone.

"Fine." I took one of the *MetroTech* pens and jammed it into a plant on my way out the door.

Michelle and Amit were under the awning, smoking. I held out my hand and Michelle shook the pack. We sent little puffs of smoke toward the office.

"Someone ratted us out."

"That marketing chick."

We made small talk, a thing I like. But they were standing too close and then walked off together. Everyone else was fucking around. I was so good, not one time with Felice.

♦

When I met Brianna, she thought my job was cool. We sold candy bars marketed to look like health food. Sometimes I think her sweet tooth was the hook. I liked that about her. She knew how to eat.

Then the sports bar craze took off and our sales plummeted. Who needs a fake sports bar when they can have the real thing? So we sat around trying to come up with gimmicks. Something else fake to replace the real thing. Our first hit was toothpaste, frosting in a tube. Mint, and it came with a chocolate toothbrush. We made marzipan smartphones that glowed in the dark. Dark chocolate laptops with licorice cords.

Meanwhile, marketing got paid the big bucks to come up with candy cigarettes.

"It's been done," I said, "and those guys got in trouble. Nobody likes it when you market to kids."

But no one was listening. Just fucking around. I could logic all day, but what did they care?

It wasn't enough to sell bubblegum sticks. Kids today were a lot less naive. So marketing came up with "Roll your own candy." Called it True Ash; it sold off the shelves. Pouches of green candy leaves and rice paper. Kids bought it and rolled it. Some rapper wrote songs.

Now marketing had disappeared, and Felice wasn't texting, and my wife was so clean.

The more I thought about it, the angrier I got. Why was I shut out of my office? Candy rolling papers weren't my idea. I just crunched numbers and signed company checks. Maybe Felice was upstairs, cross-legged and stubborn. Not texting was code for how much she cared.

I took a spin in the revolving door: my hamster wheel, energy, sparks of frayed nerve. Frank eyed me from behind his desk. I thought about pulling the fire alarm, but slowed my revolution as I realized there wasn't one. Everything was so high tech; probably an app for "Fire."

I stepped out under the awning and scanned my phone. 99¢ and a few minutes later a woman screamed "Fire" and a siren unfurled. I threw in a car crash and "Help" for good measure. Soon Frank was outside, racing into the street.

I walked past the potted plants, around the sofa, and into the stairwell. The first three flights felt fine, felt loose. By six my hamstrings and arches complained. I was panting as the tenth floor blurred.

I expected the door to be locked, so I leaned into it and fell when it opened. I'd never taken the stairs before; during earthquake drills we did shelter in place. My kids still did fire drills; tsunami drills, too. We just did earthquakes. I didn't know where I was. The room was dark, and smelled like church, or a bake sale where everyone bakes the same thing. I wished I hadn't eaten an eggwich. I should've had fruit and granola with soy.

I reached my left arm as far as it would go left, hit wall, righted myself, held the door open with my heel. The light cast from the stairwell was weak, sad, only crept inches into the dark space. The smell of overcooked oatmeal, the smell of stale chocolate chips came over me stronger. Like Betty Crocker had died.

I reached out my right hand and the wall was there too. I felt around both ways for switches. Nothing. The door fell closed behind me. Fuckity fuck. I couldn't move forward without letting it go. What was dim then became alldark, black. I waited for my eyes to adjust; they didn't. I stood there in the dark, thinking about egg sandwiches and Felice's lower lip and how easily lives like ships were sunk. The siren sounds of the fire alarm stopped. And I knew it was a matter of time.

Where lights? I willed my eyes to see, but they were useless. Fuckity fuck.

I crept along one wall. But every time it seemed the door with its thin sliver of light was still just a step behind me.

Christ, I thought. Christonacracker what have I gotten myself into. Eventually the slit receded behind me and another one appeared in front of me. I opened that door: more stairs. How... the... fuck? And beyond that, another door. I stood in the stairwell and the building hummed a little. If I listened, I thought I could hear words: *acquisitive* and *fricassee, fricative, stressless, stressless, stressless.* But it was just the tap-tapping of the air vent and the rasping of small winged insects beating themselves against the fluorescents.

Huh, I thought, ten flights up. *Industrious* fuckers. And then I thought, lifespan. They spent their whole lives getting here? Just to die against the light?

I checked my phone, but had no bars in the stairwell. Was it the same one as before? I tried the door across the way but it was locked. Had I never been in the stairwell before? I hadn't. There'd been talk of exercise walks up and down, some of the girls. But I'd never gone.

I was suddenly all turned around. And both doors were locked, fuckity fuck. And down at the bottom I'd find Frank. I didn't know if what I'd done was arrest-worthy. Not yet, I thought. But still.

My phone buzzed: a texted image from a number I didn't know:

It was a picture of me in the stairwell. Standing there staring at lights.

I should have maybe thought creepy, thought get out, thought this is the way things start to go bad in scary movies. But my first thought was: this is getting me nowhere and god do I look stupid standing here.

Another text: *try the door again.*

Which one? I texted back. Got no response.

So I tried one, the closest. It opened to a long hallway, lighted. Improvement there at least. At the end, a corner going right. The matte-white walls were scuffed and dirty before the turn. Cleaner after, dotted with a few framed photographs of beach scenes. Palm trees leaning and sea foam frozen in the moment of release. And one faded poster of Duran Duran's *Rio*. Those perfect white teeth and white skin, those lilac knives of earring, and red lips, black hair. Just as the song started up its first cycle of what I was sure would be days in my head, the fire alarm started bleating again. I'm given time, I thought. If I get arrested, well, let's make it worth it.

The hall led to the 10th floor lobby. From there I could find my way. All the elevators were closed, but one was dinging madly. It sounded like a fucking game show.

The doors to Sucrawin stood open. Everyone had left in a hurry. Desk drawers tilted. Chairs upended. The cheaply piled carpet of ill-design trashed with overturned and trampled files. The carpet was almost prettier like this.

God I hated that carpet. On hung-over days I had to look away so I didn't get sick.

Computers were unplugged and separated from their CPUs, which were nowhere to be found. Sad tails to silent machines. On Felice's desk, the candy jar had been shaken down, only grape saucers left. No one wants those. Which I wasn't supposed to say. They *were* Sucrawin, after all.

Grape saucers taste like cheap whores, Felice had said once. I got some mileage out of that. Privately though, you know.

I popped a saucer in my mouth. "Whores," I said.

On my desk there was nothing left. Only the series of 3-D boxes I had penned into the corner while on particularly bored phone calls. Penned and repenned, lines gone over and over, sometimes expanded into more tiny cubes. There was a picture of my wife from a million years ago—before, when things were a little wilder and I could pin her arms behind her. And one of the kids. God I love those little assholes, I thought. I'll never feel like I know them. But love, love doesn't have to make sense.

I'd like to love more, I thought. I think.

My phone buzzed. Another text from the same number: *get out.*
Who is this?
Now.
Who is this?

And I thought about all the times my wife got to talk and I didn't.

Sheryl? I said. Probably not, but it made me laugh to send that. On the way out, on the receptionist desk, next to the dancing statue of Purr-Purr Kitten Sour, was a manila file folder that I couldn't remember having been there before. I flipped it open. Inside, a spreadsheet titled: *The Appeasement.* I took it and got the hell out of there before things got any weirder.

♦

The Appeasement was just names and numbers. A list of them. And then some letters that made no sense at all, some kind of code.

One column of numbers was clearly cash amounts. Most in six digits, some higher, with a point-O-O after.

If they were payouts, why wasn't I apprised? I sat on the cold stone wall outside fingering the pages, chewing on my lip, and thinking what to do next. Now that I had no job would I become obsessed with this? Was that the thing to do?

I found Felice milling about, smoking her Pall Malls in the plaza out front of the building. She was standing with her skirt hiked up so high. Was she waiting for me?

"Your nails look great," I told her. Pale blue, mint green on the ring fingers. Just a little chipped around the edges.

"Were you in there?"

"I was."

"Someone said the whole building's on fire, but I said where's the trucks if that's the news."

"Company's gone. Any idea why?"

"Why are you asking me if you were just in there?"

"Because you seem to know things."

"You're talking at me. I'm just seeing where that's about to go."

"Do you want a drink?"

"Do you have one?"

"We could go somewhere."

"Why would we do that?"

Jesus, those legs.

"I want to take you for a drink is all."

"That's all?"

"You act like you don't believe me."

"Takes better game for that to work." She dropped her cigarette and stepped on it. Despite my irritation I wanted to kiss her stupid mouth. What would the world be like if I just did that? If I was a person who just kissed a beautiful mouth that was in front of me?

"You don't happen to know Marketing's name?" I asked her.

"Why?"

"I want to ask her what happened. She doesn't show up one day and then things are just over."

"Isn't that how it goes—someone stops showing up?" Felice turned around and started walking. After a few paces she stopped. "Legal would know."

"What?"

"The name. He knows everybody."

♦

I got in my car and turned on the radio. Took me ten minutes to admit to myself that I didn't care what was happening in the world right now. Did I ever? I switched to something Top 40, all Cristal and ass. But then the hour hit and it was "throw-back" whatever and Jodeci came on and it was like high school again and I was at Homecoming, standing in the dark and twinkling gymnasium where I never asked Sandrine Calleo to dance.

I knew where Legal lived, but didn't have his number. I had been there once when he'd moved. A new house. I was as shocked as any that he'd had a housewarming and invited me. He was friendly, but in that distant way. I don't know what I expected, but I wanted to know what beer he would buy. Bridgeport, the I.P.A. and then something local. That had seemed about right. And then the almost empty bottle of Laphroaig I saw in his kitchen that I knew he hadn't moved with. No point. There were only two or three fingers in there. Had he drunk a whole bottle of good whisky in the week and a half that he'd lived there? In any case, he was in a much better pay bracket than I'd ever be.

I didn't have his number. Could I just show up? And then Nelly's "Country Grammar" came on and I felt compelled to move, to do something. What? I popped the trunk and got the 2-liter bottle of Vodka of the Gods. With the label ripped off it looked just like a bottle of water. I hoped. I took a few drags until I got clear about what I had to do, got back in the car and rolled up on Legal.

I knocked on the door and some dude answered. Someone I'd never seen before. Nice shirt, nice tie. Had I got the wrong house? No, there was the brass lion knocker on the door, the sun dial on the lawn. And I realized: I didn't know Legal's name either.

"Is Legal here?"

"I'm sorry?" the young man said.

"I'm—"

"Sucrawin?"

"Sucrawin, yes."

"Hold on a minute," he said and closed the door all but a crack. I heard him walk off a few paces before yelling *honey* into the cavernous house. Gay? The thought had never occurred to me. Good for him, I thought. It was hard not to admire the young man's intensely good looks. I've always prided myself on my ability to separate sexual attraction from attention to the detail of attractiveness. I was in no way *interested,* for example, in boning this young man, but GQ would not have turned him down. As he led me into the house, I even admired the way his slacks fit neatly over his ass. *Good for him.*

Legal's boy led me into the kitchen where Legal was standing with his hand in some pot. He shook it out and I heard some scratching. "Lobster," he said by way of explanation. He had a white apron tied around his waist, a yellow Polo shirt uncovered, a spot of red (wine? blood?) near his navel.

"You don't know my name do you?"

"I did once," I said.

"Doctor," the young man fake-whispered in my direction.

"*Doctor?*"

"Yes," Legal said. "My father loved the nickname 'Doc' and thought the best way to make sure of it was to name me Doctor."

"You're kidding."

"He's not," the young man said. "Have you ever thought about *your* name? Or, like, the name James or Douglas or Karen? Where they came from. It's all just sounds."

"This is Nurse," Doctor said.

"He's just kidding."

"It *is* what I call you."

"Henry," the young man said, and held out his hand.

"Hank," Doctor said. "I like Nurse Hank better."

"Of course you do," Henry said, leaving the room.

"So what's this about? Do you want a drink?"

Laphroaig? I thought, eying the brown liquid in his crystal tumbler.

"Whatever you're having."

He poured it neat. Tipped his glass, raised an eyebrow.

"I'm trying to get ahold of Marketing."

"And?"

"I don't know how to reach her."

"Or know her name?"

♦

Taylor Swift (Marketing) lived in a brownstone halfway across town. Is her name really Taylor Swift or are you fucking with me is what I asked Doc. Nurse Hank laughed like he'd heard the joke before. I asked also about the payouts, but Doc wouldn't tell me about any of that.

I went up the steps, knocked, and no one answered. I sat in the car and ate two energy bars, UpBeet & Butters. Who knew beets were so good for you? They made my mouth red; the almond butter stuck in my teeth. I thought of zombie films, all tough sinew and gore. Every time, I thought. Didn't help to wash it down with Red Bull. I stuck my tongue out. Red. Rinsed with Vodka of the Gods. Still red. Jesus. At least my breath was clean. Like mouthwash.

I heard Joan Rivers used vodka as deodorant.

A car pulled up and Marketing got out. Jeans, a pink t-shirt. Before today it'd been nothing but dark pantsuits, blue or gray or black.

"Taylor?" I got out slowly, not wanting to scare her.

"No one calls me Taylor."

"Are you—"

"Alison. It's my middle name."

And it was then I noticed the resemblance. Why it had never occurred to me, I don't know. The brushed out blonde finger curls, bright blue eyes, dark eyeliner, the semi-opened sparrow lips tinted ruby red, sweetsoft voice, and the cutest fucking nose.

"You look like Taylor Swift," I said, stupidly. "Is that a stupid thing to say?"

"Is that what you came here to talk about?"

"No."

"Are you going to murder me if I let you in?"

"I'm just worried about my next paycheck. Is the company going to start up again or is it over?" Suddenly who she was seemed important. That song about being trouble was starting to fuck with my synapses.

"I don't know what I can tell you."

"Why did you get in trouble?"

Red lips, wry smile.

"Who are you?"

"I was made in the late 80s. A product. Born fully formed and kept on ice until the future was ready."

"What does that mean?"

"There are hundreds of us."

"Fully formed?"

"Yes. Born at 18."

"And you never age."

"Only how we were programmed to. Which is gradually. Something you'll never notice in your lifetime. I have a half-life of 300 years."

"Why not go on forever?"

"The planet doesn't have that long."

"But do you sing?"

"I can."

"But, so…"

"Yes, she's one of us. One of me."

"Why marketing for you?"

"There's one of us in each profession." Then she told me about subliminal messaging, which was effectively banned in the 80s after soda pop got caught with sex on its mind. "Even though research on action priming shows that subliminal stimuli can only trigger actions one plans to do anyway."

"Was Sucrawin using subliminal messaging?"

Marketing nodded. "Just on the candy cigarettes, the new kind, the rolling kind; it was something we were trying. If it's truly subliminal, you can't get caught. I've been using it my whole career. Mostly on soda and political campaigns. After the SEX in the ice cube debacle (not my campaign), I decided to show it could be done. I was just showing myself though. I never let on to the executives or anybody that I was inserting anything below the threshold. But I was."

"You were?"

"With the candy and the rolling papers, kids were just supposed to think it was cool to roll your own tooth decay. Somehow kids started snorting it though. And then getting mixed up in harder stuff—bath salts and methamphetamines. Everything went up their noses. Sales were through the roof, but kids' faces were losing the game. Gummed up sinuses. Some kids were filling other holes, betting on a quicker high. I won't go into what a mess that was. No one ever figured out the problem. I can't even say I did. They couldn't pin it on me, but they asked questions."

"Why are you telling me this?"

"Because you're the only one asking."

"You don't think I'll take this public?"

"You won't. You're not that kind of guy."

I just looked at her.

"My job is to know people. It's what I do. You're not a guy with follow through. Besides, I'm assuming you'll want to be on board when we start back up again."

"We're starting back up?"

"We just need a little rebranding. A new logo will probably fix most of the mess."

♦

A year later Sucrawin reopened with a new focus: everything gluten-free. Beans, nuts, dried fruit, beef and salmon jerky.

Things that wouldn't have gluten anyway.

I came up with the pitch. Walked away with *Employee of the Year.*

That was part of my appeasement: a trophy. There were other things, too. Things I asked for and got. Some of them NSFW.

Brianna and Felice get along just fine.

THE EMERALD ROOM

Let's take the children out to the woods and leave them.
—Beckian Fritz Goldberg

I never meant to quit my job.

At lunch I walked to South Lake Union and ate pho from a food truck. My lunch break stretched, oozing over the hour line. I took a little walk turned long, past Amazon offices and the Gates Foundation, past BioMetro and MetroTech, sidewalks busy with workers like me. Pot smoke wafted from bushes under the overpass. I followed Denny to Capitol Hill, past bearded boys kissing in front of taxis for hire.

I was three Facebook degrees from most of the city, but didn't recognize a single face.

When it got dark, I ate an energy bar and drank the rest of my water. Thought about smoking, then remembered I'd quit. We had a bet at the office—me, Amit, Michelle. I'd collect tomorrow if I wasn't fired.

Sometimes not getting fired felt really hard, a shadow job trailing my first. I unwound by writing angry letters to City Council about the Woodland Park Zoo. Sometimes in my cube I gnawed on my arm; how much worse would I feel if I was an elephant? Stress in captivity. Pacing, self-harm, waggle of the head that scared children.

I walked past light rail until the sky rained stars.

Easy enough for a white girl to live here, with my treadmill desk, free pizza on Fridays. But I had this dream? Where I talked to people? Snail mail, wet signatures, landlines. Real time.

My phone sulked in my pocket and I thought about Brianna. How she invited me to go power walking, the fastest thing to do in Bothell. I had a crush on a housewife with kids and a sweet tooth whose husband worked three cubes from mine. While I walked, the city built buildings around me. It would be so easy to become someone else. Brianna seemed like that kind of girl—wound up and waiting for someone to save her.

I still had her number. *Whazzup*, I texted.

Who's this?

Felice

My therapist said I didn't know how to make friends. But it wasn't that; I just wanted to fuck them. That was me, all needy and sticky. No reply. I wasn't surprised.

Then a bubble appeared, like our phones were still thinking.

Olive Garden for lunch tmrw?

Noon's my break

Sounds good see u there ☺

I hadn't planned on going back to work the next day. I thought I was quitting pretend-unconsciously, taking such a long lunch break that they'd disable my keycard. But now I had a lunch date, or at least a lunch something. I had to go back, just so I could leave.

♦

At lunch the next day I learned that Brianna had changed her first and last names when she married Brian. Just to be sure.

"Sure of what?"

She picked the walnuts out of her salad. "You know how gay people can get married now? And how bakers have to bake gay cakes or they'll get fired? Brian and I didn't want anyone to think we were having a gay marriage. We wanted things to be super traditional."

Twelve children and counting. Off with her head.

"Traditional how?"

"We totally waited! I wore white and stuff. But then Brian couldn't get my garter off and I sprained my ankle when my bridesmaids spilled rice."

She wasn't eating her croutons, so I ate them for her. The waitress kept offering cheese.

"How well do you know Brian?"

He hits on me constantly. "We're in the same department. Three cubes away."

"Are you married?"

"Nope."

"I could fix you up. My brother works for Microsoft."

"Thanks, but I do okay."

The cross between her breasts disappeared into her shirt. She sat back and played with her tennis bracelet.

"Look, Brianna, we don't have much in common. I'm just trying to make some new friends, is all."

"Me, too."

"You have lots of friends."

"You talk like it's the 1950's. You don't know what my life is like."

"Fair enough. Why don't you tell me?"

"Brian comes home from work and wants a blow job. I get on my knees for him while the kids scream in the other room, and then I just want to eat chocolate, but he tells me I'm fat."

"That sounds like a nightmare."

"Mostly I'm bored. I thought marriage would be about sharing a life, but we have two lives and they don't overlap."

"Do you want a divorce?"

"How would I support myself? This is my job. It's what I do."

I leaned over the table and untangled her hoop earring from her hair.

"Sorry." She blew her nose in her napkin. "I'm talking too much about myself."

"Not at all. But I gotta get back to Sucrawin." I don't know why I said that, if I'd even go back. I had to punctuate the conversation somehow, put a period on something with so many commas, ellipses.

"Of course." She stood quickly, dropping her purse. Lipsticks and breath mints and used tissues scattered under the table. At the center of the mess was her pink rhinestone cellphone. Out of guilt I picked up the tab.

♦

When I got back to my cube Brian stood, hovering.

"Hi Felice."

I turned my back and toggled the mouse. Photos of candy filled my screen. I could feel Brian breathing behind my chair. I clicked and typed, toggled and clicked.

"How was lunch?"

"Pure Olive Garden."

"Bri said you had fun."

"Fun was had."

"Wish I'd been invited. We should have lunch, too."

"Ain't gonna happen."

"You can think it over."

"The answer is no."

"Bri said you need friends."

Someone's ringtone boomed a Taylor Swift song, one flavor of trouble with an autotuned swirl.

"That's Bri's ringtone. You guys are like twins."

The ringtone kept yammering, but no one picked up. Stupid, stupid—

The sound was coming from my jacket. I reached into my pocket for Brianna's phone.

Sometimes I do things almost on purpose, with just enough unconsciousness thrown in to keep it all on the down low. This was one of those times. So I'd stolen her phone, and maybe I'd meant to. The pink of it, spangled, hot in my hand.

I couldn't call to give it back. But I could show up on her doorstep while Brian was busy.

"Actually, Brian, I'd love to hang out. Drinks tonight? How about Siren downtown?"

He was so excited I almost felt guilty.

It took 55 minutes to drive to their house.

♦

Bothell was a suburb, but it had a rural feeling, and not in a good way. Not deer and pine trees, but pick-ups and gravel. Brianna was sitting on the porch of their faux colonial when I pulled into the driveway. She was wearing a bathrobe and smoking, hair tangled up in a knot on her head.

"You're a lifesaver," she said, before I was out of my car. "I totally knew you picked up my phone. It's got all my pictures and Facebook stuff."

"Facebook lives in other places."

"Not like in here." She tapped the phone to her chest and wrinkled her nose. "Did you drive all the way from the city?"

"I was in the neighborhood."

"Come on in. Brian's got a late meeting."

Bowls of rainbow-colored chocolates. Lace-edged curtains. Twin armchairs. Cream shag. We moved into the kitchen, backlit by green. Tendrils snaked from hooks on the ceiling. The room smelled like forest and crinkled like silk. Maybe the rain in Seattle started here, poured from a watering can shaped like an elephant. Brianna moved from plant to plant, talking to leaves in a sexy voice.

A cat emerged from a cluster of ferns. I bent to scratch and got scratched, pronto.

"That's Ash. And there's Smoke, behind the schefflera."

I sucked on my wrist to stop the bleeding.

"He bites and scratches. It's what cats do."

She seemed different in the emerald room: tougher and fonder, less of a wife. One of the palms needed repotting. She took off her ring to dig in the dirt.

I glanced at my phone. Six texts from Brian. He'd invented emoticons to express his dismay.

Where R U?

Fender bender

Lemme come get U!

Be there soon

Another minute, and Brianna's phone rang. I snuck into the bathroom, not sure what to do. The bathroom had a red balloon theme, with embroidered hand towels and balloon-shaped soap. What if he told her he was supposed to meet me? But he wouldn't, I reasoned; he'd already lied. I splashed water on my face and checked my email. The soap smelled delicious. I wanted to bite.

Brianna was holding a bottle of wine when I got back to the kitchen. "Red, white, or spritzer?"

"You're sweet, but I've overstayed."

"Brian just called. He drank too much at dinner. Had to get a hotel. You should crash for the night."

"Does he do that a lot?"

"Tomorrow's the weekend."

She was right. The room was so green.

Brianna shrugged. "I should check on the kids; they've been quiet too long. Back in a sec."

◆

I had done this once before, fallen for a woman. Two-toned skin on her chest, all burn and cover, and a round splotch on her cheek. From sun, she'd said. I like things that don't match. One girl tall, one short; my hand on her head. One blonde; brunette. One girl who was girl every chance she got; one who wasn't. One who liked to put her mouth around things; one who liked to be inside. It wasn't true that all cunts were alike. One loud; one calm, serene, a slow flame. Then laundry.

Sometimes I forgot whether I wasn't still in it. Whether the cats got in my way when I got home, got between us. Whether there would be excuses to make, making up to be done, before the sheets opened and I tried again. Sometimes I forgot whether I was supposed to or wasn't supposed to when I shoved up at the bar with my wedding face on. "Is this seat taken?" Was it? I shrugged. Something in me always available. I never went home with any of them; it never got that far.

One left handed; one always right. One top; one bottom. One likes to swim; one does dishes with gloves, mops with boots on.

Inside the bathroom, outside of the stall. Another one and another one. It got to where I couldn't see a row of sinks without thinking where her ass would go or his and how dirty the floor would be to my knees. Men without pants on; women all buttoned up, popping. Or the seat was always taken. I shrugged, phantom to the heat inside me. Things went farthest election night. Republicans took over and I never went home. One key in the lock, changed lock in the door, cats circling blowsy leaves on the porch.

"Brianna, can I be honest with you? I want to do your laundry."

"What?"

"I mean, I want to dirty your sheets."

"What do you mean?"

"With you."

"With—?"

"Have you ever?" Ever what. I just kissed her then; words useless, turning on themselves.

♦

Back at work on Monday. Brianna and I hadn't talked since. Brian brought donuts and stood at my cube's opening until I took one, until I bit into it, until I murmured the good.

"How was your weekend?" he asked.

"It was okay." Long is what I thought. Long between thoughts. I got stuck on one and couldn't shake loose: the smell of her hair.

Monday was an economy of gestures, of reinvented small talk. Somehow everything I said seemed new. Talk of the new restaurant across the street. What kind of drinks I liked when I went out. I would try new things from now on. I would find that shampoo. Could I ask him? Would Brian know? What if I texted her to ask? Brianna, tell me what shampoo you use so I can get it, wash the cat with it and go to bed feeling closer to you. Did I love her? I didn't love her. Did I want her? That much was true. What was it I wanted? My teeth on her jeans. Feeling the wet sex of her through denim. How slick she was with wanting she couldn't admit to. She didn't look at me. She didn't look at anything, eyes closed tightly to keep her in some other world of her making while she was with me. I'd been there before. Sometimes you come out of it, just a little. Sometimes one eye will open the other.

I asked Brian what were her favorite flowers. He didn't know and didn't ask why I wanted to. It didn't matter to him: girls, flowers, why wouldn't that be small talk. "My mother liked daisies," he told me. That sounded like sunshine, overcompensation for misery to me. But I didn't say so. "Did she?" I said. I didn't ask about what blooms witnessed their wedding. Something traditional, I thought. I thought maybe to send her some callas, that most modern-looking of blooms, all economy and swoop. Deep and long, both phallic and its opposite.

I settled on regular lilies. A mother's flower, I thought. Some virtue, the sweet smell of things before all this, sticky hands, shrill cries of want, rote sex, indistinct desire, lack of desire. Desire everywhere, filling rooms with wants not hers. In the checkstand: wants. A pack of gum or candy cigarettes. Jessica Simpson loses baby weight again; she looks down at her thighs. In the bedroom: down. In the bedroom hands and knees take on different meanings. In the kitchen: hot dogs and mac and cheese. And: those shoes, I want those not these, those pants, not these, two socks alike, and where is my, where is my, where is my. The endless stream of wanting that comes from joining lives. The overlap and subsume. The institution. Lawn care as weeds grow and grow; flag up mailbox the checks go out. More. The next door boy with his shirt off doesn't eye her. Girls come and go when that mother is gone. Some need met. And she's always home. Lilies smell like: *then*, teenage girl perfume, a boy's clean shirt the body odor pushes through, an easier time, the first wet mouth at soccer camp, church organ and the space between rooms. Of course lilies are also the bloom of bereavement, what funerals have on hand to cover the death scent of formaldehyde and clothing rotting to the forever lying-down form of this newly, dearly. And Easter when things get up again. When we're promised things we only see from the outside. I want to go again, she thinks. I want to start it over, she thinks, not do it different, but *feel* it while it happens to me.

I sent her lilies and she didn't text back. I sent her roses and she sent them back.

"No way to explain," the flower shop matron said.

The delivery girl said Brianna said. "Trouble."

What did you expect?

And then it happened again. The late night out for Brian, subterfuge. That Kathy in accounting. I knew he'd be out, had set it up myself. I'd heard Kathy was into free drinks and would make out with anyone. I got Brian riled too before it. Short skirt shorter, rolled at the waist, caught in a drawer. A lot of leg when he came by. I pretended I was presentable, ate grapes slow while he fingered the change in his pocket: a tell. Boy, Kathy was going to get it, daiquiri by daiquiri.

I showed up unannounced at Brianna's with three pizzas and the latest Pixar to keep the kids busy. What I wouldn't do.

"What are you doing?" she said.

"Planning ahead. The wine is for you." A ten-dollar bottle made to look thirty.

"You can't just stop by," she said. And then some version of "no." But I just walked right in. I told myself a no with clothes on and no contact was different; I wouldn't push it too far.

"One drink," I said. "And then I'll go." And in that slight relenting, the almost happy to see me, if only to break routine, I saw her pants on the floor, felt the trick of her bra clasp come loose in my hand.

Paper plates out, the kids settling in. Caustic coma of cheese and we were on again. My hand inside her shirt, then her pants. She was already there.

"You can't say you don't like me," I told her.

"I can say anything I want." And it was silent after that, only breathing fast or slow under the high-pitched hum of the flat screen in the other room.

And then the next week it happens again. And she won't speak to me after. And this time I force her to talk, threaten to show up on a Tuesday when I know *he'll* be home. We go back and forth for a few days talking and talking about the meaning of it until one of us gets bored or until one of us says I love you and then there's nothing else to say.

A WOMAN WITH A GUN

I'm cooking dinner while you're researching sex offenders.

"Are you sure?"

You nod. "Eight blocks away."

I turn down the heat, wipe my hands on my apron. Toss egg shells into the compost bin. Our city has laws about food waste recycling. Asparagus stems, heels of whole wheat.

Sometimes I hear things when I'm home alone. In the green of the kitchen, my hands in the dirt. You're in Tacoma, Oly, or Portland. Stuck at the office. Always at work.

You asked for a blow job and I asked for a gun. I thought I should ask for what I wanted, too.

"Don't keep it loaded," the first thing I learned.

But what's a gun for if the bullets are gone?

♦

After you left, I threw the chainsaw bear out the window. It landed roughhouse in a pile of leaves. We'd bought the bear on a trip to Bow-Edison. Stopped for grilled cheese, went home with Pierre.

"But Pierre is your dog's name," my sister said. She called once a week to not talk about Mom.

"It's flattering."

"For the dog or the bear?"

"I mean about Mom. How is she?"

"The same."

I hung up and stared at Pierre among leaves. Above him, a plastic owl guarded the deck, glowering at birds who might fly into glass. The sun was shining in androgynous stripes, rain rustling beyond the bamboo.

When the rain swept in, I carried Pierre onto the deck by the guardian owl. Pierre-the-Dog barked at this new, old thing invading his territory, littering leaves. I let Pierre smell Pierre. Then we went inside and shook off in the kitchen.

That first night alone I slept with the lights on. Soon like a cat I'd see in the dark.

◆

My sister called again on Monday.

"How's Mom?"

"The same. How's Steven?"

"The same."

When I hung up I tried to remember who Steven was. Nine or ten years ago. Some guy in a bar. My sister changed my boyfriend's name, variations on S: Stanley, Sam, Sarge.

It bothered you, the inexactness. The way things disappeared in the curves of our mouths.

"We're family," you said. "Tell her to remember."

But we were a family that chose to forget.

◆

"How's Mom?"

"She and Harlan are living together. Dad's photos are gone. How's Simon?"

"The same."

◆

The happiest moment of my life was in an alley, California poppies and peonies freckling a dumpster off 19th and Mercer. You pressed me against the brick back of a stranger's apartment. You smiled your private smile and later we named a stray dog Pierre.

Your name wasn't Steven or Simon. When you dumped me, I cried at my cubicle desk. We worked together. We still worked together. After you left, I brought Pierre to work. He squatted, protective, at the door of my cube. Not really a door but the space between walls. Not really walls but gray pasteboard partitions.

"What's up with the bear?" Amit asked, trending.

"It's named after my dog."

"What's your dog's name?"

"Pierre."

Amit looked both ways and stepped into my cube. "It's like a movie star trailer in here, Michelle."

Pink shag rug, striped swivel chair, scented glitter pens, and a disco ball. In the drawer where I kept envelopes and sticky notes, a gun.

◆

I couldn't get used to the kick back. I couldn't get used to the small smell of fire. The way the metal washed light over my fist, over my wrist. I couldn't hit cans. I couldn't hit picture frames. I couldn't hit the stuffed bears I bought from Goodwill.

I could scare away birds. Both with the *blam* and with my curses.

The sky was a pink-orange wash of nature's effluvia. I saw entrails everywhere. Everywhere I saw death. But when I held the gun it was heavy. When I fired the gun it shot skyward. I was no threat to anything really. I was disturbing the peace.

"Put the bullets away," my sister said. "Have it just for show."

I put the bullets away. But I touched the gun all the time. Sitting on the couch knitting a three-armed sweater. Sitting on the couch drinking raspberry tea. I had it pressed between cushions and I pet it there. Sitting on the couch with popcorn and a movie, I kept it out on the table. While in the bathtub I kept it under the sink, too far to touch, but with the snub nose pointed out. Its little nose was a comfort. In the kitchen while cooking I kept it out on the counter. "Good little kitty," I said. I didn't know why. In bed, of course, Kitty slept on my pillow. At work, Kitty slept in a drawer. I stroked it while on the phone. I stroked it when Amit stood at the opening of my cube. If he asked what I was doing, I pulled out a scarf. I kept the scarf in there just for that purpose.

"Petting that scarf again, eh?" Amit asked.

"It calms me," I said.

"Feels like fur?"

"Feels like something alive."

♦

That afternoon we had a fire drill or earthquake drill or something half-interesting. Everyone panted down ten flights of stairs. Amit and I waited it out under the awning, smoking.

"Looks like Brian's in trouble again."

We watched through glass doors as Brian yelled at security, pounded his fist on Frank's desk, and jabbed a pen in a fake potted plant. He stumbled outside in our direction. Held out his hand for a cigarette.

We sent little puffs of smoke toward the office.

"Someone ratted us out."

"That marketing chick."

"You're creative. You should be up in arms."

My mouth twitched thinking of Kitty: in arms.

I took a bus downtown just to walk around. My purse felt light. My purse felt empty. I had nothing to touch. After rifling through gum packs and wrappers, tubes of lip gloss, some vacant notebook, a couple dry pens, I spent the whole ride fingering the zipper on my jacket pocket. I watched men spread their legs and furtively paw at their crotches. I watched women try not to notice, hands in their laps, legs crossed at the ankle.

Amit liked me, so I thought about that. But we worked together. But who the fuck cared.

Would my sister remember a name starting with *A*? Would Amit be into the stuff I was into? What about Kitty? How would she feel? Then I remembered Kitty didn't have feelings. Kitty was *it* and wanted to kill.

◆

Blam, etc. I shot leaves off trees. I shot *X*'s on fenceposts. Gunpowder perfume. I needed a concealed weapons permit, so I used Sucrawin letterhead and wrote one myself:

To Whom It May Concern:

Michelle is a hard worker. She's the heart and soul of Creative here at Sucrawin, and she needs a gun. Michelle is more cooperative and productive when she has a firearm. She's also available to defend company property, such as non-dairy creamer, the water cooler, and the candy jar on Amit's desk.

Sincerely,
A Woman With A Gun

I printed three copies: one for me, one for my drawer at work, and one for Amit. I put Amit's copy in a sealed envelope inside a locked metal box and threw away the key.

"This is for you," I stopped by his cube. "It's a present and also a mystery."

"How come it won't open?"

"It's not supposed to. But if you want to have drinks, I'm free after work."

We met at 7 at a bar on the Hill. Soon he was giggling and I was morose.

"My mom's having more sex than I am," I said.

Amit made a face. "No senior sex talk."

Then he invited me back to his place, an overpriced studio in South Lake Union.

"Amazon dorm," he said, punching buttons.

I left before coffee could make us a thing.

♦

My sister called to not talk about Harlan.

"Mom calls him her lover. What should we do?"

"As long as they're using protection, she's fine."

"You talk to her. How's Susan?"

"The same."

♦

I couldn't get used to the rug burn in Amit's apartment. Sneaking out before he dressed for work so he wouldn't ask me which shirt to wear. All of his shirts were blue, were white. Kitty slept tangled in a scarf in my purse.

My sister called to ask about S. I kept telling her A, as if A was his name. We wore our alphabet down to deep letters. I thought about B: what came next by design.

♦

C for the man calling out to the dolphins from the University bridge. "Fuck you, dolphins!" *D* for the dolphins.

"There aren't any dolphins in there," I said. "It's freshwater."

"Fish can't talk about fish," he said, shaking his fist. *E* for the exchange I'd rather forget.

F is for fish, freshwater, fist, for friendly fire. I pawed at my girl, my Kitty wrapped tight.

G is for grace.

A girl with a gun is a strange thing, a tender thing, a thing coiled with potential. I wanted things with Amit to stay light. I wanted one hand on my sternum; it didn't have to be his. I wanted another hand on my wrist, loosening my fist, wrist to wrist, digging in. I wanted velvet lawns in other cities, clean lines, cross-hatched designs. I wanted ink spots in all the right places, the illusion of safety. I wanted ten-dollar bills, and the double-metaled shine of Canadian coins. I wanted to shine. I looked at the traffic around me, at the man still yelling down, ripples on the water's surface, on the dirty oil lines and flotsam of Starbucks coffee cups, holiday red. What would it take, I wondered. The man flipped me the bird, grabbed at his dirty blue jeans, started walking towards me. What would it take? A gun could go off or not go off, the world would be the same after. The same one thousand trillion trillion molecules in a body lying down. The same six cycles of breath in a body standing over. The same 93 million miles to the sun. The same light eight minutes gone.

50TH ANNIVERSARY OF A MAN-MADE LAKE

This morning, dog balked at a buck
in the carport. I unfasten things
by the side of the road. 6am call.
Gray man and his flatscreen. Tender
with wrinkles, pre-Stonewall
wrists scarred. I take him while we watch
the news because this is how news
lets itself be surprised. Fluff piece
at sunrise. I grip what I can. The only way
I'm ever touched. Some combustion
in the center flares, then holds, collapses.
Some dim lens widens, contracts.
Cat backed in a shelf, all purr. Watches
the lube bottle, us. Some sound of slapping,
the TV hums, volume down, pictures flit:
the blonde, the lake, strip mall, healthy
balloons hit by wind, blonde sheen of bubbles
bursting in the bath. We barely fit,
so I step out, uncork a towel, cock the remote.
Control what I can. The buck stared down
leash, dog, and day. The day blew

morning coffee cool. I am, I think, watertight.
Sweat rolls right off. Airtight. Sweet smoke
he won't inhale. One hit, I puff up again.
Cat backed. A purr. Same slap.
The blonde. Some hint of boom.

TO KEEP YOU CLOSE

I'm at a party, watching your mouth form the question everyone asks. The question no longer interests me. Instead I watch your lips crease into the slightest smile, then curve askance in apprehension.

Are you planting them in humans?

Yet.

Are we planting them in humans *yet*? Because the answer is some-day; it's just a matter of when.

The answer is yes.

I say no, and explain the kill command: once an object is chipped, we track it; once we've tracked the object to its destination, I key the command to kill all traces.

I keep my face calm.

I say no. I say never.

Our microchips are meant for objects stacked on pallets on the bulky bruised arms of a forklift.

Our microchips bleat as objects migrate.

Our microchips send data across distances, preventing loss.

Loss = sadness.

Therefore, our microchips engender happiness.

◆

The party isn't meant for me, and neither are you, although your lips are still moving.

If you really looked into my eyes you'd see code, ferrying your thingness home.

♦

I live alone; the streets are full of us. Seattle's mostly water, like any body. Tech's new blood, and we flow uphill. Sometimes I work all night, binging on coffee and e-juice, tapping keys until spoken English feels quaint and out of date.

I can follow anything you buy.

Take that pair of shoes, for instance. Embedded in their soles is a chip I coded, code to track shoes from factory to warehouse to store.

The kill command comes when the item's sold. The goal is kill when the object's yours. Our tracking ends; the trail goes dead. You go home with the thing and a murdered chip, lodged somewhere inside.

Trust me.

I shut it down; I kill the code at the retailer's cue.

Can I turn the chip back on?

Can I start tracking you again tomorrow, soles treading uphill as you walk to work? As you flee a custody suit or an abusive spouse? As you shed a name you never meant to keep this long?

♦

Your lips move. The party changes mood. We're drinking bourbon and the salmon's gone. We're vaping clouds of candied ash. It's late, too late, until it's early. I think about rogue objects, ghost chips that stop blinking on elaborate maps. How they disappear without even flickering. Faulty chips sometimes stop working, but people also learn to dig, to probe into the body of the thing they've bought.

In the meat of your thigh, in the crease of your wrist: prick of an injection and I'll follow you home.

♦

Dating's difficult when you're keeping secrets. The nondisclosure forms keep piling up. Sometimes I imagine them old school, on paper. Stacks of sworn promises never to tell.

Some companies make you sign on for at least a year, with a five-year window specifying you won't work for another company like theirs if you leave. There's no reward for obeying the laws of noncompetition, just punishment if you try to compete. So I walk around with all this knowledge I can't share or use on my own. I keep accumulating reams of data. When I buy a girl a drink, I worry code will infect our conversation. I try to keep things simple, light:

What's your favorite smell?
Can slugs see in the dark?
Favorite noxious weed?
What's your birthmother's birthday?

After the second date, if we get that far, I bring her to an abandoned amusement park off the highway between SeaTac and Federal Way. I've always wanted to kiss on a slide, and there are so many plastic tongues littering the graveyard of the water park, pool bone dry, ribs of the Ferris Wheel a ladder to the stars which long ago I thought I'd study, before I met Jasper and the chip on his shoulder.

None of the girls call me back.

I start over.

Slide right, slide left.

Hello. Be mine.

I just want to whisper my secret into someone's ear, cellphones off, naked and chipless, far enough away from South Lake Union that no one will catch us and kill me, which is what they'll probably do if I tell.

But I'm getting ahead of myself.

My name's Elvis. And you?

I watch your lips move, answering a different question.

◆

Tech interviews are usually high fantasy mixed with mundane snarls, like driving a red sports car through rush hour traffic. For every nitpicky quiz about substrings or quantum electrodynamics, there's a question meant to showcase your problem solving process-slash-personality. When I interviewed at Sucrawin, every other question was social. I laughed through my nose and spilled coffee on Jasper's treadmill desk, gestures meant to reassure them I scored low on ego, high on geek. Nerdaciously I slumped and stuttered. I never saw Jasper's face. He was bent over his phone and laptop the whole time.

As I left the office, a future coworker handed me a pen.

"Is it chipped?"

Felice smiled. "Everyone asks that."

"Meaning yes."

"Do something illegal and see."

I went to the zoo, a place I hate, and cut a hole in the fence of the aviary. The escape was spring, the kind of spring Seattle doesn't have, all flashes of color and speed and the smell of dirt and worms and sunflower seeds; all sky and black gash in the blue as dozens of birds formed a flock and flew in a V toward Miami or maybe Cuba, now that it was open for business.

Actually, I left the pen on the Metro.

I have no idea if it was chipped or not.

CAKE

So I find a bag of sugar in the cabinet and text to say I know she was here, coffee with sugar and cream in the morning, sugar a thing neither one of us keeps.

You text back emojis: fireworks, house.

I don't know which one's meant for me.

Your girl at the market. Your girl with red nails in a fake fur jacket, smoothing her hair with a practiced gesture, shoplifting chocolate and peppermint soap. Your girl in stonewashed jeans and neon high-tops. Your girl drinking whiskey in a bar with carved booths.

I see her on billboards and magazines: girls who look like that, who mean what she means. How perfectly keyed to get down on her knees.

I see sugar everywhere.

She's the muse behind your art. I'm your broker, half a wife, selling your brushstrokes to men with money who want to hang girls on the walls of some bank.

◆

I meet Jasper at lunch to discuss the Cezanne. She's there in the lobby, your brushstrokes familiar, each shadow a secret I've watched you protect.

I only broker art I like. Some of my peers say it limits me, say the work I present to clients has a certain sameness. But I won't watch someone spend millions of dollars on a painting they couldn't pay me to hang.

People ask which came first: your fame as an artist or mine as a broker.

I say nothing.

I say the girl in the painting.

I say the girl in your paintings is always the same.

◆

So much money in South Lake Union. Seattle's been panning for gold all these years. Now here it is, and the new rich are kids. They don't care what they wear. They don't care what they drive. Their houses are bungalows, craftsmen with gardens. They grow their own kale and build roosts for chickens.

I moved to Seattle in 1995, tired of New York and too edgy for Boston. It looked like a vacuum to me, and it was. I started with Microsoft and networked from there. The way to get someone to spend money on art is to make them think one is better than two. Technology's all about duplication, the proliferation of identical parts. These kids own everything twice or ten times. They have multiple partners in business, in bed. High art's unique, one flawed piece someone owns. Old school, like heaven. Suspenders and guns. Lately the kids are all nostalgia. They name their boys Stanley, girls Mabel or Nell. Landlines, tobacco, straight razors, gin. Candy cigarettes rolled up in their sleeves. It's the old days, however far those days go.

I make them hungry for the bright, hot thing.

To own an object, someone's time on your wall.

I don't have a website. Strictly referrals. By the time we meet, they're hungry to buy. It's a passion I cultivate, grooming each buyer. Like a vampire I knock and they bare their white walls.

Jasper was different. He heard my name from a friend of a friend, but pursued me because he was selling, not buying. He'd invested early, before the first crash. Played it safe, nothing post-1940. When we met fifteen years ago, he was ready to sell those cumbersome masters. I was tuned in to the tone of the new. Ready to risk, to place bets on unknowns. I invited him over to our house by the water. Our walls were covered in your early oils. Back then it was me, my face over and over. My shoulders, my hands. Back then I was your muse.

I'd prepared slides of emerging artists. Jasper sat silent, eyeing each piece. The room faced the water, boats on Lake Union. Two bottles of red, some ridiculous cheese. Above the window was one of your first: a long, narrow canvas of lace flecked with dirt. The suggestion of thigh, my skirt always lifting. Jasper stood up and approached it, entranced.

Artist?

Catherine.

Your partner?

My wife.

He bought five of your pieces, five pieces of me.

When I think of nostalgia, I think of those days. I ask if you love her and you shake your head no. Why don't I believe you? Because art doesn't lie. Because my rope's gone missing from the gardening shed.

The submissive buys her own rope.

Because you lied about me.

Because ten thousand's gone missing from our joint account.

So you ask her to do things, and Sugar, she does, but she comes with a price, and I've paid for too long.

I tell you I'm planning to ask Sugar to lunch.

She won't eat in front of you.

What will she do?

Look, you're my wife. She knows I'm committed. She has to respect you; that's one of the rules.

I didn't consent to your affair with this girl.

If you loved me, you say, *you'd love this in me, too.*

In person your girl was tall, with an awkward slouch and long dark hair. Short striped skirt. White shirt, red bra.

I paid for her coffee and ate cake while she watched.

◆

Jasper asked to see your new oils. I met him for drinks at Lou's on the Hill. You may have forgotten how I look in heels, but he watched me walk in, and I walked very slowly. He kissed my neck when he took my coat, and kissed me again with my coat back on.

You'd started a series: your girl on the lam. In one of them Sugar stood on a slide, arms outstretched, as if ready to fly. Carnival lights greened the night sky like stars.

He paid me in cash.

I stiffed you by half.

[*]

After

the ceramic

kitten

merger,

I

smoked him

out of
the concrete

play

room

SOMEHOW ALWAYS GETTING IT RIGHT

I want to say to you, "tell me how to be and I'll be that." I want to say, "you won't catch me standing in the rain." But you come home and I'm in the driveway staring at the sky, staring at the negative space between tree branches, wet to the bone and getting wetter.

I tell you I broke three bones as a child: my left ring finger, my right thumb, my left arm. But I didn't break any of them, other people did. Is this a useful distinction?

When you get home, new tires on new gravel, new house and new yard, it shakes me out of myself, reverie or thoughtlessness. I used to think I could get high from breathing regular air deeply if it was cold enough and the breath deep enough. Then I learned this was true. There's a jump-start effect to a few deep breaths like that. Maybe why the doctor told me to take deep breaths when—

"What are you doing?" you say. Something that doesn't seem like a question. What do I answer? Standing here? Getting wet? Feeling her? Waiting for you to get home?

They buried her in a communion gown. She'd never had communion, but it was the prettiest thing she owned. Like a tiny bride is all I kept thinking. Like a tiny bride for Jesus or some fucking shit fuck you universe fuck you God and Jesus.

My thumb is now double jointed. Sometimes I can't do anything until it cracks and sometimes it won't crack.

"I just thought of something," I say. Then something about the trees and the owl. And you say, "come inside." I say okay and still stand there getting wet and you shake your head and beep the car locked and go inside. I want to say I'm trying as hard as I can. But at what? And I'm afraid you'll ask and I won't have the answer again.

I got my first bloody nose in the first grade. Yes it was a fight. Yes I won. I wanted someone to tell me once, just once, that I was scrappy, but no one ever did.

You turn the porch light on and it feels like a statement. But one I can't decipher. I think of all the lights I've ever seen go on, sunrises and everything. Mostly I think of concerts and all their colored lights. I like them because there's no utility. Most are just for show. What is gained from seeing Dylan in red and then green and then blue? Would I be understandable if punctuated by the right light, the right hue?

My therapist says I miss her. I think it's something else.

New house, new yard. New porch, new door. I'll open the door and you'll talk in circles. Not about us. Not about Cora. Just random things that happened at work.

♦

Brown eyes. Wide nose. She loved cats and sea gulls, skateboarding and gum. Cora ran so fast she won races at school. Favorite color: pine tree green. Favorite song: whatever was playing. She was eight years old, took Route 7 to school. Got off the bus four stops early that day. The gas station at the end of Fairview sold strawberry milk and candy cigarettes.

She was crossing the street, school bus flashing red blinkers. Someone in a hurry. Someone on their cell.

The day of her ending, something happened to language that keeps on happening. Suddenly there were words I couldn't say. Not that I didn't want to, just that I couldn't. I started a list because I could still write them down.

argyle
spruce
gymnasium
puncture

For a while I drove to Cora's school every day. I followed the bus to make sure her friends got off at the right stop. Then I started following them to make sure they went straight home. Then it seemed easier to ride the bus. To eat lunch with her friends in the lunchroom at school.

I asked to enroll. I did; that's true. I had trouble with language and time on my hands. You were farther away than you'd ever been.

In the end, everyone wears a blindfold; isn't that how the story goes?

"What story?" you said.

The story I wrote.

♦

Your girlfriend lived two hours south, on a hill in a city bisected by bridges. It was something you did: a hobby, a craft.

"Like knitting," you said. "Like jogging. Like pie."

After Cora died I wanted to know everything about you, to make up for the giant hole in my chest. So I met the girl you played with on Fridays. She was brittle and pretty, with Bettie Page bangs.

Sometimes I write stories in my head because I want the ending I want, and that's the only way I'm going to get it. My therapist says I have abandonment issues. Issues with women. Issues with men. I told my therapist that the girl with Bettie Page bangs looked like a supermodel. Like what holds up a bra at Victoria's Secret.

My therapist looked confused. It was getting harder to tell the truth, and now here I was, trying to explain my spouse's fetish to a stranger in loafers. How you were sometimes someone else with someone else, but never with me. How I'd asked for you to be that someone with me, but you'd said I was someone who couldn't see you. How I'd seen glimpses and felt more alone. How the girl with bangs kept part of you gone.

My therapist gave me glazed therapy gaze. "All of us have myriad selves."

Cora was dead; she had only one self. You had so many, and I had to share.

◆

When I got home the fake owl was lying in the grass, gravel bleeding from a hole in its back. Cora loved the fake owl. Carried it like a baby. Fed it rocks to keep it from tipping. It was supposed to scare real birds away from our windows. Giant glass rectangles reflecting pale green.

The week we moved in we lost three birds. The first bird died, turned bone on our porch. The third fell outside and we dug a low grave. But the second bird was trapped inside. Came in through the chimney, got stuck in the pipe.

I was home alone. You'd gone to the store. Cora had soccer and I had this bird. I opened the door to the woodstove and cowered. When it flew out it flew directly for glass.

The bird and I spent an hour chasing reflections. It smashed into windows, fell dead to the floor. Rose up again, bleeding. Perched on the bookshelves. We had cathedral ceilings and it froze on the beams.

In retrospect, everything's rosy as I toss a blanket over the bird the very first time it strikes glass. I cup it gently under the blanket and it doesn't protest as I carry it outside.

In real time it flew into windows, fell dead, fluttered to life just before I could save it, then perched somewhere I couldn't reach. As I approached it flew toward the windows again.

When I heard your key in the lock, I cried.

You walked with me to where the bird lay after its latest strike, legs stiff in the air.

"It's dead."

"No, bird legs just do that."

But you were bending over, touching its wings. Its tiny chest wasn't breathing or stirring.

The driver stopped. Got out of her car. A witness says Cora was breathing, was talking. The driver tried to pick her up, because panic does that, does the wrong thing. Panic is when the right thing won't save you.

When I think of the woman who killed my daughter, I call her *my* daughter.

You say *ours*.

We say *love*.

For eight days after we cleaned spots of red off the shelves. Books battered by birdwing had to be set right, smudges on the wall, smudges on windows. For eight days after I visited the stain in the road. At home I sat upright, unmoving for hours. I stood on the lawn and looked down at little graves. The stones Cora had placed there, the dead flowers crusting brown. "They had lives," she had said. "They had goals."

What did she know? A spelling bee she wanted to win, but *argyle* took her down in the fourth round. A boy she wanted to be or to touch, she cried on the couch about how soft his hair was. "Isn't she young?" we said. "Isn't she *precocious*?" We started the talk about birds, about bees. But she'd already learned it from YouTube.

For eight days I sat shiva, scarves covering mirrors. You peeked through to check your hair on your way out the door. "We aren't even Jewish." But I didn't care. Eight days I let things burn on the stove while I walked out to the road.

Eight days. Then followed her friends at school until the principal told me to stop. Teachers told me to stop. Parents pleaded with me. Teachers and parents and secretaries lined the office. No one said intervention, but that's what it was. Pink backpack high. Awkward brace face high. Glossy cherry chapstick high. Smell of Pantene on a juvenile head high. Her pillow had lost her scent and I stood in the road.

♦

After, I walked to the mall on the other side of town. Stared at small creatures in carts, small creatures in strollers. And the ones holding hands and the ones not holding hands, wandering racks unattended.

It started with a little girl named Rebecca.

"I'm going to call you Cora."

"Rebecca," she said.

I took her hand, sticky from something, red on her face. Her mother was trying on swimsuits.

"Lollypop?" I said, wiping her hand on my jeans.

"Sher-bert."

"How was it, Cora?"

Cora shrugged.

"Do you want another sherbet, Cora?"

"Rebecca."

"Do you want another, Rebecca?"

She shrugged.

"How old are you?"

She shrugged her shoulders.

"Five?"

She said, "I think so."

I was imagining her taller, a little bit older, a little more red in her hair.

"Rebecca," her mother called from inside the shiny shut door we'd carefully moved away from. "Rebecca, get over here," her mother said, then opened the door.

When I returned home that night and you weren't there, I carved a space for myself in the living room couch. I covered myself in leaves and fell asleep watching lights blinker on and off in neighbors' houses through the trees. I woke up underwater, or I didn't wake up at all. I saw you above me, the wave or riding on it, immersed but not drowning. Thrashing arms, but not drowning. You dance so much it's hard to know if you're struggling at all.

◆

The second one wore a green coat with fur around the collar and looked nothing like her. Not the right age or hair color, not the tea olive smell of her skin. Asked no questions, did not count off-color cars in the parking lot. "Orange," Cora used to say, "look at that. Bright orange and silver orange. Two lizard green. One pink one."

"Look at that pink car," I said to the girl. The license plate said KITTY. The girl said nothing.

"Look at that green one."

Nothing.

"Go back inside," I said. "Go back." And when she didn't, I realized I had to let go of her hand. "Go," I said. And she did.

And there was the one who cried, and of course I returned her immediately. "I'm so sorry," I said, over and over, "I'm so sorry," while the car dragged itself back to the fire lane in front of Target.

And the one who ordered French fries but wouldn't eat them. "I ordered you fries."

"I don't want them," she said.

"You said you did," I said.

"No, I didn't."

And the one who called me Auntie Grandma.

And the one who could manage the Honda's sticky buckle herself.

And the one who sounded right, knew all the right movies, but had dark curly hair. It couldn't be her. Would I have to wait until Cora was reborn? How long would that take, and should I look for her younger? Pull her from cribs or from strollers? All I wanted was to hold her hand, stop seeing her lifeless, stop seeing that stain in the road. What used to be our daughter. I wanted her giggling at the antics of squirrels, her stories of alien abduction. I wanted her babble about dinosaurs, all of the names and all of their faces crayoned into the wall. I wanted to sing all those songs from all those terrible movies. I wanted her back again. Her hair and her breath, her pillow, those candy cigarettes, ring pops, licorice. How she loved Brussels sprouts, but wouldn't eat green beans, loved onions, but not peanut butter. The way she demanded jam all the way to the edge of her toast. I would have given anything to make her breakfast.

And then there was the one who bolted when the car stopped. Ran off like an animal uncaged across a dark parking lot.

I could get none of them home into the next-prettiest dress, none with their hair just right, none to call me mama.

♦

Counterpoint to the rain and dark clouds, inside a haze of synthpop, Erasure and Tears for Fears. Here, in this room the light won't find me, here, the walls all tumbling down. Maybe all I needed was to be in this with someone. Maybe all I needed was for you to come home. Between the curb and the weeds, between the car roof and the dashboard, the endless road running at me, movie of a world. Yet still in my car I'm invisible. Yet still in my car I continue unseen. Hand on the stick shift, a bag of Oreos, some little jacket, some lock of hair.

ASH

After you quit, you became one of those people. Nothing matched the taste of ash. You'd snatch at smoke in strangers' mouths, stamp cigarettes with a twist of your heel. Now and then you went too far, stealing candy cigarettes from children. This went on for months until you started smoking again.

You quit tennis lessons; you quit taking the bus. You knit half a hat to match all of my eyes. You quit jobs and religions, broke leases and vows.

You quit everything, but you never quit me.

Because I knew you were born to quitting, I built quitting into my expectations. I started joining things for both of us. I brought home disasters wrapped in bright scarves.

♦

Your affair's name was Kayla. Her twin's name was Kylie. They were dental hygienists with spray tans and fake breasts. They snapped their gloves with the same practiced gesture. Beyond a few questions, I wasn't jealous at all.

"Why Kayla and not Kylie?"

"Kylie plays for a different team."

"Which team is that?"

"The one that's no fun."

When you quit Kayla, you sulked a sulk I'd never seen before. Your lower lip twisted and twitched. Then one morning you brought me coffee in bed, your smile placid, and you were easy again.

♦

After the wedding you broke all of our dishes. You wanted to start new, you said. I caught you fingering forks and spoons, daydreaming meltdown, metal on fire.

♦

When you didn't come home, I wasn't worried. You'd gone feral and vanished before. But weeks of no calls and your zig zag tattoo. Threads from your sweater. Your last dental records.

I told the police it wasn't you—the face under the sheet, the impossible leaving. Like a cat, you always returned. I trusted you to work some kind of magic.

♦

Mirage-time.

I saw you everywhere—the arboretum, Georgetown, First Hill. Once I swerved in Belltown traffic when you waved from the balcony of a shiny hotel.

♦

Someone called 5 times, no message. Hitting redial I called Green Lake Dental. Kayla had the voice of a woman who put her fist in strangers' mouths.

I said your name and listened for clues through the static of a bad connection. But she said she'd heard nothing, and I chose to believe her. Asked her to lunch, which led to three things.

The third thing was searching her apartment while she was in the shower. By this point I believed that she had no idea where you were, so my search was mostly to understand where you'd been. It wasn't even fun to snoop. You were omnipresent as her twin. I half expected you'd had children together, Becky and Buster, life formed from clay.

♦

Sometimes I missed you. Chocolate seemed to help, but some nights it got so bad I downed shots of cough medicine and lay in bed with a cloth over my eyes. My dreams were fantastic then, three-legged animals with pink scales and blue claws.

We continued texting as if nothing had happened:

Pick up cupcakes?

Pick up beets?

But of course my phone could talk to your phone, my fingers tapping both bright screens.

♦

I quit my job and found another just like it, the kind of thing you used to do.

It rained for 56 days straight.

Green things hung from the overpass, dripping.

♦

Cleaning under the sofa cushions I found your datebook, annotated in Swedish. You didn't know Swedish, so you made it up: odd words in fake places, new names on lost streets.

♦

When you were easy, I thought I knew you. Your smile looked natural and your wrinkles relaxed. I thought I could tell what you were feeling, read your face the way you read mine.

But although I knew you better than anyone, I knew you less well than you knew me. It wasn't that I wanted to know to know you better. I just wanted you to stay.

ALL NIGHT DOG

Sometimes I drove all night to see you. Then we walked my little dog.

You were two different people. I gave your first, best self your name, but called the self that pocked in angry splotches by another, shorter name. When you were best, you looked at me like I was prairie forever. All wood smoke and pant cuffs and wildfire spring. When you were angry, you looked at me like I was the changeling. I never knew which you you'd be when I showed up, pulse still set to the highway, road rage tangling my hair like wind. Not until kissing did I know for sure. The way you kissed changed depending on who you were and how you saw me. When you were angry, I tasted spearmint and ash. Happiness tasted like cherries and weed.

You had two names, two sudden selves. I needed a second, secret life to match the two in you. I should've been a spy, or crossed the border with Canadian flowers stashed in my trunk, blooming quarantine.

APARTMENT ABOVE

After Amit left, I got weird again. Went back to who I was before. All the old ways of being alone came back overnight and then that's who I was. Eating soup out of the can, walking to the grocery store in my pajamas, staring at the ceiling for hours, arranging each cup in the cabinet just so. Everything I'd learned about myself with Amit vanished, like he'd had the blueprint to our lives and now I was sleeping in the woods. Except sleeping in the woods might be romantic, but this was just low, ostracized from the tribe.

I gave it six months before dating again. After three dates I adopted a cat. It seemed easy enough to brush her fur and shake fish-shaped kibble into a mouse-shaped bowl. The one thing I couldn't do was name her. Cats and dogs, hamsters and ferrets, all named "Brooklyn," "Hamish," or "Peach." Waiting for something better, I called her Kitty. Like ash on the tongue, the name lingered. Kitty was small and soft, a pale yellow ghost. At night she slept curled in the crook of my knees.

My apartment was tiny, a daylight basement with bars on the windows. I couldn't tell if the bars kept people out or kept me inside, but the result was the same. I made myself leave the apartment at least once every other day. Since I tended to lose track of which day it was, I kept a schedule on the door. Eventually I lost track of the schedule, but its floating gold stars wouldn't unpeel.

I'd always been an addict of the weird: restlessly counting pink cars or stone birds, picking at scars or cracking my thumb. Now I had a new addiction, soft puffs of sugar and vanilla-tinged sweet. Candy cigarettes in a bright pink package. I sucked and then bit, catching coy glances at myself in the bathroom mirror. Liked what I saw: red lips, black bra. "Take that, Amit," I thought, pretending I was an old-school movie heroine, stranded on tarmac, waiting for my old-school Handsome to whisk me off in his convertible. Amit did very little whisking. "Take that," I thought.

He'd left me for another woman, the way it happens when someone is done.

An affair isn't actually about the third party, my best friend reminded me. An affair is about what's unspoken and wrong. Still I couldn't stop seeing them tangled together. It didn't help that Amit kept painting the scene. They'd met when Kylie started art modeling to put herself through dental hygiene school.

"So you paid her to undress," I said.

Amit just smiled.

I wanted to be someone's muse, someone's mistress. Instead I stayed home in my pajamas, texting, talking to Kitty, too uptight to vape.

♦

The noise from upstairs woke me one night not long after I adopted Kitty. I sat up in bed, disturbing warm cat. The sound echoed, ripples through plaster. Heavy, like barbells or a human body. Bump, crash. Then no more sound. So back to sleep, and by morning I'd forgotten the whole thing.

Like so much of Seattle I telecommuted. Every morning I woke to a queue of documents filled with grammatical errors. I worked for a candy company trying to break into the energy bar market. Thus, free candy. Thus, anxiety. My colleagues-in-candy developed ideas like UpBeet (*The Only Energy Bar Made From Hemp Milk and Beets!*) and Purr-Purr Kitten Sour (*Grab a Pussy To Go!*). The idea lab was definitely more interesting than correcting comma splices and misspelled nouns.

It was one of the days I forced myself to go out. I pulled a skirt over my pjs and put on a wool hat, although it was hot. I figured if someone saw through my disguise I could pull the hat low, puff on my smoke.

Leaving my apartment involved the lobby, which involved a pool table, flat-screen TV, and numerous papier-mâché giraffes. For the first time ever, someone was holding a pool cue and lounging by the awkward chairs. I recognized my upstairs neighbor, who also worked for Sucrawin.

"You have a cat," he said.

"Yes."

"We're not supposed to have pets."

"Says who?"

"Landlord."

"Why do you care?"

"I don't. You have pajamas under your skirt."

"They're stuck."

"They don't go with your clogs."

"I like comfortable footwear."

He gestured toward my hat. "It looks deliberate. Like you made an effort."

"I did." I offered him a candy cigarette. "I'm going to the store; do you need anything?"

"Is your cat's name Kitty?"

"How did you know?"

"I'm Elvis."

"I'm Taylor."

"You're at Sucrawin, too."

"Marketing," I said. "You're a brogrammer."

"Funny. Do you play pool?"

I took a cue from the wall and stretched over the table.

"Wow," he said.

"I'm good."

"I see."

"Play sometime?"

"You know where to find me."

♦

At the store, the card reader wouldn't eat my card, so the cashier had to type numbers into the computer manually, sighing elaborately, like it was just so hard.

"I'm sorry," I said.

"You need a new card. The chip is scratched."

"Thanks for letting me know."

"You really need a new card." He leaned in and whispered conspiratorially, "The chips have eyes. They see everything. If it's scratched, it's because someone scratched it."

"I have a cat."

"They're watching you." Then he looked at the guy behind me, fuzzy beard and suspenders. "Next in line! Would you like a bag?"

That night the noise happened again. This time Kitty and I both sat up, and Kitty clawed my arm trying to escape when I tried to hold her. I turned on the light and watched red beads of blood form in a line on my arm. It only hurt a little, but looked so dramatic I was pleased. It made me think about Amit and Kylie, whether he cut her, what it was he wanted from her that I wouldn't do.

The noise was definitely coming from Elvis's apartment. I decided that if I went upstairs and knocked on his door, it counted as an outing, and I didn't need to leave my apartment for three more days. Never mind that it was 2am. Code monkeys kept strange hours. He was probably lifting weights and watching porn, or playing asphyxiation games. Maybe I'd save his life by cutting off the plastic bag. This made me race upstairs, pajama bottoms dragging on the gray-brown carpet. When I got to 2F I stopped before knocking. What if he was with some girl, or guy, or both? Before I could knock, the door opened, and Elvis walked out.

"Hi, Taylor."

"Hi, Elvis."

"How are you?"

"Fine, thanks." I looked down at my fluffy slippers. "Were you playing asphyxiation games?"

"No, I was playing Apartment Golf." He lifted the pool cue in his right hand. "I invented this game? Where you use a pool cue like a golf club? And hit the balls against your furniture. It's called Apartment Golf. I've got an app set up and I'm testing it. If I can sell it, I'll make enough money to quit Sucrawin."

"That sounds kind of dumb."

"I know. But I need to take the cue downstairs now. Excuse me." I followed him down the stairs.

"Taylor, why are you following me?"

"I'm lonely," I said. As soon as I said it, I knew it was true.

That's how we started. He kissed me in the stairwell, hands on my waist. We played pool, and I invited him over, and we fed Kitty some hairball treats because she had hairballs. Gold stars glowed on the door, on the ceiling. We kissed again, sitting on my couch watching the Space Needle on a postcard I'd tacked to my wall. It was almost like having a view.

TWINS

My parents gave me two middle names: Taylor Nadine. On my birth certificate, my first name is blank, horizon stretching away from recognition. I grew up in two households, answering to two different names, smoke screen of fog while I code switched between them. When I was younger it seemed normal. The older I got, the more it divorced me, until I decided to pretend I was twins.

Taylor lined her lips blood red while Nadine wound orange yarn around her fingers until they turned blue. "Look," she said to the lady behind the counter at Knit Wit, "my finger is about to fall off." When Nadine smoked, Taylor ratted her out, crumpling the pack, poking her finger through smoke rings, singing that refrain about trouble from the beginning.

In this manner, like outcast others before me, I orchestrated a life I could bear.

DEVOTIONS

We spent the day taking pictures of cars. It's one of Nadine's obsessions. Old rusted out cars, hubcaps missing, bumpers falling off, doors left permanently ajar for passengers or drivers who would never come. She says she likes it when form finally wins out over function like the abandonment of the American dream.

There's a junkyard not far from Nadine's house. She lives 12 miles from me, out 522 past the intersection that keeps killing teenagers, just over the city limits into Snohomish.

Sometimes she sits in the field next to the yard, reading books and watching the men who work there reel the cars in. Sometimes people drive them in—clunking, clanging, smoking—but usually they're pulled in on the back of a tow truck. The junkyard has its own truck with a silver-blue cab like the bay's wintry chop or heavy rain clouds. And the back of the truck, when it's empty, looks like it's hauling Jesus' cross.

"I think I fell in love today," Nadine says on the highway while driving back to my house. Her hair is blown forward on her face by the 65 m.p.h. wind when she turns to me. "That Chevy," she says, "was really something."

"The blue and white one," I say, "the one with the wings?—I mean *fins*." I often have trouble speaking around Nadine, even after all this time. She's all hair and hands, and has long long legs. I never know where to look when I look at her.

"No...wings—I like that," she pauses like she's considering the weight of this in her mouth. I see her tongue move over her teeth behind her lips. She does this when she thinks. "It wasn't even rusted out too bad."

"No," I agree, "it looked pretty good."

The only pictures I had taken all day were of Nadine with that car. Nadine rubbing the dirt off the chrome bumper with her forearm, Nadine sitting on the back of it. Nadine stretched out on the abused upholstery in the backseat.

Nadine was the one who took the pictures mostly, pausing only seconds to frame shots. Sometimes when the camera hung off her shoulder she would frame a potential shot with her two thumbs pressed together, fingers held up like a makeshift goal in a game of tabletop football.

I brought a camera too, my mother's Minolta—a nice one, and lied when Nadine asked if I knew how to use it because I wanted her to show me how.

Nadine knew about a lot of things. I liked her to tell me things I already knew so I didn't have to pay so much attention to the words.

My mother doesn't really like us spending time together. Mostly it's because of the way Nadine had smiled when asked about whether she went to church regularly or not.

"No," Nadine said, "my mom let us decide when we were ten if we thought our relationship to God should be public or private."

"Oh." I could tell my mother didn't know what to say and wanted to touch the crucifix at her neck by the way her hands leapt from her lap a few times like fish out of water before she settled them.

"I don't really go at all," Nadine said. "Just Christmas sometimes with my grandmother."

"I think that girl is a bad influence on you," my mother had said after Nadine had gone home.

"She's *spiritual*," I said.

"Oh no she's not."

I wasn't sure how much my mother disliked Nadine. And I still worried a little that she could read my mind sometimes. She told me once that mothers had this power. I still haven't completely gotten over that. I worried she might see into me when I looked at Nadine—so I mostly quit bringing her around to the house. And my mother didn't even know that Nadine had kissed me in the movie theater once while the credits were rolling and everybody else had gone. I remember the smell of the theater—popcorn and piss—and the way our shoes made smacking sounds on the gummy floor every time we moved them—but I don't remember what movie we saw.

Neither one of us said anything after the kiss. I didn't know what to say. I hadn't realized I wanted that until it happened. As soon as her lips were gone I forgot what they felt like and wanted to remember. Nadine just shrugged, picked up her empty cup and someone else's discarded popcorn tub and made her way into the aisle. I followed her without saying anything, and wondered if God would forgive me if it was love.

We ride back most of the way in silence along the highway. Nadine lights a cigarette and turns the radio loud, but not so loud that one of us can't say something over it if we want to. Halfway to my house, in the middle of the bridge that goes over the reservoir, there's a minivan parked on the shoulder of the road and an older woman standing in front of it staring at the car's flat tire.

"We're going back," Nadine says. She's looking into the rear-view.

I don't say anything, but I'm thinking how dangerous it is to stop. The shoulder is narrow, traffic fast and I'm late getting home to my mother. I stare at the water in the reservoir, then at Nadine's hands on the wheel, her knuckles clenched white as she U-turns at the gap in the median.

By the time we circle back around, someone else has pulled up behind the woman's minivan.

Good, I think, we don't have to stop.

"We'll just make sure everything is okay," Nadine says as she rolls in behind the two cars. I want to grab her hand and tell her not to get out. Two trucks hauling stone rattle past and Nadine's car rocks gently from side to side like someone quietly saying "no."

There is a man bent low at the flat. His body is poised somewhere between the pose of Christian prayer I know and the pose of some eastern religion prayer I've seen on TV where everyone is curved forward with their palms out before them pointed all in the same direction. The man is bent over the wheel, his body turning as he turns the metal x in his hands, turning to get the bolts off the sad circle of tire. His hair looks damp and covers his face, so that I can't tell how old he might be.

When we get out of the car we meet at the end of the hood and walk together like a scene in a movie. I wonder if she notices times like these, when we are actresses and move like we get paid to do it.

I can smell rain, the smoky odor of wet pavement. The highway and shoulder are still damp from an earlier downpour. I glance at the water, wind-chopped and sloshing below, without getting too close to the edge.

The man waves an arm in our direction as we approach. The gesture is vague and wide. He could be signaling hello or indicating something in the distance we should turn our attention to. I shudder every time a car or truck approaches. I turn my back and wait every time, wanting/not wanting Nadine where she is so close to the road. To be protector or protected, I often can't decide. I am waiting for the accordion crush of our parked cars. My calves feel weak when anything drives past. The wind from passing cars lifts our hair. It floats over our heads like the hair of a body dropped into deep water.

The woman steps out from behind the man, stepping around him carefully. "I think we've got everything under control," she says, "or at least *he* has. Wow, what a place for a flat." Her neat hair is gray and pulled up in a bun, under control save for a few errant wisps. We're reading her lips mostly, her words are pulled from her mouth and tossed over the rail toward the air and water there, or sucked over her shoulder in the rage of a passing semi.

Behind her, inside her car, a small dog barks, furiously swiping his claws at the window. His hot breath steams the glass and his high-pitched insistence punctuates the roadside's rough movement of air. The dog moves, scratching and sliding from side to side. He barks and barks, scrabbling at the window. I put my palm up to the window before we turn to go. I close my eyes and feel the tremors against the glass.

WAYS OF NOTICING NADINE

1.

Nadine says we come from water, so toes test temperature. She's such a know-it-all, but she does know. Mother says eat eggs. Father says *cocktail cocktail cocktail* like a neon sign. I'm lonely all the time so I brought Nadine to live with me. She sleeps under my bed like a dog in its collar. If I get lucky someday she'll crawl onto my pillow. We'll breathe the same air back and forth. That would be sharing something really good.

2.

Nadine says he's one of us. Fur same as hair same as skin. This is where we come from. We crawl into the woods, climb on each other's backs, bray. We stumble in leaves. Make babies out of milk. Branches above us like God's eye in church.

3.

She cleans and polishes them for men. Carries spare bullets in her jacket pocket. At least I know I'm not the target. *Nadine,* I say, when she squints one eye. Crosshairs snare doves, snare deer, snare gray hair and wing tips waiting on the 4:09. *Get lost,* she tells me. I walk while she rides.

4.

We brought the changeling baby to the fire. The baby changed the fire, but the fire changed faster. After, we stood on hind legs and whispered nightmares into lace. *Let go,* muttered the creature in freakspeak, teddy bear to its bare chest, diapered and best dressed in unholy long tresses. We had to set it free or moonlight would suffer. We took its bottle and its view of the teat. Everyone thought we were hiding a bomb. Photos on the mantle hatched smiles gone wrong.

5.

Green was the girl's favorite color. Green skirt, green purse, and green for the railings lining the boat cutting slices in the green-black sea. Two girls tousled until the bigger one won, holding shorty down on the bench until small sister caught fire with the unfairness of it all and slapped. A soda to soothe her. A trip to the bow to meet sea spray head on. No mother in sight, and what use father, with all this boat lurching up to dock? Below deck, passengers idled their cars while two girls in green ducked under the railing. Hit the pier running, disappearing into the May Fair crowd. Stashed the empty wallets in a storm drain off 10th.

6.

Don't look at Nadine. Look at the chair, how its blue fills the room. Look at the gold frame and the patterned rug, woven with one deliberate imperfection. Don't look at Nadine, holding gloves as if they were hands, as if she were finally sure of someone. Look at the mirror, oil on canvas. Don't look at her necklace, bruise you swear you can hear above her heart. Wine dissolves into sun on water, sails passing through the spill, splitting gold into shards of blue glass, glass table filling with the afternoon you found yourself on your knees before Nadine.

7.

The world imagines us in pieces, couch cushions catching our hair. How will I keep anything of myself after revealing my flaw? There were declarations, oranges, tweed. Air so still. Candles burned straight up, dissolving into the nothing we become. Like Tuesday's ashes, still, I quieted every thought.

8.

The night Frank tries to strangle Nadine she breaks a glass on his shoulder. So here we are in Harborview—beige walls, window looking out at an airshaft. Fingering his collar. *Betcha think you're clever.* Kiss and release. Sweet smell of disease. They make me explain: *I was cooking. I'm clumsy.* Later he buys me a burger at Dick's. *She don't have to know.* I feed him grease. By the time the bill comes he's strangling me.

9.

Try telling that to Frank. Nadine climbs to the roof for dramatic effect. From here she can see the drugstore where she was raped and the house where she bought her first pregnancy test. Oranges hurry out of their skins on trees that smell like smog. She slips out of her skirt over a six story drop. All she owns: Frank's t-shirt and a pack of menthols. Swinging her legs over the sill, looking past flip-flops to the sidewalk, she counts baby carriages and dime bags, pinstripes and mercenaries. Clicking her heels she transforms Frank's brownstone into a field of blue cows doused in second-hand snow.

10.

They put it all on the lawn. Went through the books this way, dishes, socks. Everything sodden and green. No question about the knickknacks she'd collected from a lifetime of dead relatives: snow globes, Limoges, menagerie of porcelain creatures cracked, Girl Scout figurines, skirts' green faded cream.

11.

He'd never killed before. His car did it for him. Pulled over onto the dusty shoulder and waited while the life light dimmed. How to bury the corpse and know what it knew? He would become the bird, instinct through sky, stealing flight as her bones lay grounded. But nothing happened. There was the road, and the car, and headlights passing, not giving a second glance to what lay dying. After, he said I want to know what my hands can do. That was how it started. Water, pastel, oil, tattoos. He inked his best work between his lover's shoulders. Each wing glowed black against pale blue, stars reaching down to her legs, which were broken. She'd never walk again. This had happened to more animals than he could count. Still he had to try it out. Let each number roll inside his mouth, lucky number until he spit it out.

12.

We didn't know what it was. It was like the pictures we'd seen, but there's always a difference in person. The legs in their angular way seemed so harsh, so focused on bruising the earth. The rest of it moved slowly, like something so damaged it would never get right. I want to touch it, you said. And then I got a little closer. I want to touch it, you said again, and we held out our hands.

13.

Nadine curls Rachel's photograph into a spyglass, peers at the flowering cherry in the arboretum. A three-legged cat mewls at a bowl painted with fish and bones. For weeks now a man has been coming and going. A woman buries her ring at the base of the tree.

14.

Every time she moves she gets a little bigger, a little farther from her mother, a little closer to the end. This is where it happened. The story of this room fills highways and bars. The only quiet place in the world is right here, the one place no one imagined you'd go. Someone's painted the walls and ripped out the carpet. In the closet, a forgotten corner of sky.

A FISTFUL OF KEYS

(a play in one act)

The stage is dimly lit. Nadine is lying in bed alone.

Nadine: Brian? Brian, is that you?

Brian: (enters in a mask, walks over to Nadine and pushes her down on the bed.)

Nadine: No! Stop!

Brian: Shut up, you fucking whore. (slaps her)

Nadine: Stop! Get off me! (struggling) No!

Brian: Don't you talk back to me. Don't you say one fucking word. (slaps her) Shut up. Just shut the fuck up. (slaps her) Jesus. (stands up) Jesus Christ. (walks away from the bed, takes off his mask)

(pause)

What the fuck are we doing here, Nadine?

Nadine: (sighs)

Brian: Sorry.

Nadine: So you got yours, but I didn't get mine.

Brian: That's not what I'm saying, sweetheart.

Nadine: Is this about Brianna?

Brian: I was thinking of Catherine, actually.

Nadine: Fantastic. Let's each think sad thoughts about the other person's spouse and feel guilty enough to shut down our fun.

Brian: Speak for yourself.

Nadine: You don't feel guilty?

Brian: This isn't fun.

Nadine: What's not fun about it?

Brian: For one thing, Wyatt's in the other room.

Nadine: He's sleeping. And he's 6 months old.

Brian: You don't think attachment parenting might be worth a try?

Nadine: Now? You want me to pick him up and not put him down now? Are you going to participate in this little experiment? Because he's your son, too, even if—

Brian: Keep your voice down.

Nadine: If no one knocks on the door when I'm screaming "Stop," no one's going to barge in and ask you to take a paternity test.

Brian: Catherine might—

Nadine: Might what? Listen through the nannycam? Suss us out with a private detective?

(pause)

Besides, Catherine already knows.

Brian: Jesus.

Nadine: It's fine. She doesn't care.

Brian: (stares at Nadine)

Nadine: What?

Brian: (stares at Nadine)

Nadine: Okay, she cares. Okay, she got out of the car when I stopped at a light and walked 4 miles home. And isn't speaking to me. And sleeps on the couch.

Wyatt: (crying)

Nadine: Oh, honey, I'm here. (goes into the other room) Shhhh baby. Shhhh little baby. I'm here, mama's here, I got you. There, there.

Brian: (yells toward the other room) Should I be dad now?

Nadine: He doesn't have a dad. He has two mommies.

Brian: And we're cheating on one.

Nadine: Speak for yourself. I told you, Catherine knows.

Brian: That's not the same as consent.

Nadine: Fine, then you walk out that door. Take a goddamn Uber to work.

Brian: I will.

Nadine: And don't come back.

Brian: I won't.

Nadine: (comes back into the room) Why are you still here?

Brian: My feet are stuck. You put a spell on me.

Nadine: Please.

Brian: That's right. Say it again.

Nadine: Please? Please, darlin'.

Brian: (walks over to Nadine and kisses her passionately.) See how sweet it can be? Why's it gotta be rough all the time?

Nadine: Because too much soft feels rough to me. (They kiss again, softly at first, then Nadine grabs his hair and pulls his head back.) Because it's sweet with Catherine. Rough is what I want from you.

Brian: (steps away from her) Every creature in its cage, waiting for the zookeeper to unlock the door.

Nadine: If I'm the zookeeper, yes. (laughing)

Brian: A fistful of keys, Miss Chatelaine.

(pause)

You have no idea how sweet I can be.

Nadine: I've had enough sweetness with Catherine to last a lifetime.

Brian: Really now? So you'll only unlock me for play.

Nadine: Brian, we've been through this before.

Brian: (Walks over to Nadine and kisses her. They kiss for a minute, then Nadine pushes him away.)

Nadine: Stop. I mean Scrabble.

Brian: Is "Scrabble" our safe word?

Nadine: What good is a safe word if you forget what it is?

Brian: Why would you use our safe word for kissing?

Nadine: Because I'm late for work. I called and told them my car broke down.

Brian: Because it did.

Nadine: Yeah, but this isn't about a breakdown, is it?

Brian: Maybe. (starts laughing)

Nadine: (laughs also; walks over to Brian and kisses him passionately)

Brian: Bingo! (laughs)

Nadine: (laughs)

Brian: Monopoly! Candyland! Risk!

Nadine: Bingo was funny. You should've stopped there.

Brian: How did you tell her?

Nadine: I just did.

Brian: How did you tell her?

Nadine: How did you tell Brianna?

Brian: (silence)

Nadine: Thought so.

(pause)

My work is done. I'm a free woman.

Brian: You're still married to Catherine. Nothing free about you.

Nadine: I'm more free than you are. Freer. That sounds wrong; is "freer" right?

Brian: How did you tell her? I want to know, so I can try it on Brianna.

Nadine: You'll never tell her.

Brian: Yes, I will.

Nadine: No, you won't. Not unless something crazy happens, like we're hit by a semi and you have to explain to your wife what you were doing in a rental car with a sexy stranger.

Brian: Unless you die and I survive.

Nadine: In this story no one dies, okay? We told a few lies, a few feelings got hurt.

Brian: In this story does Catherine know my name?

Nadine: We were at the zoo, you know, with Wyatt, and I told her.

Brian: Does she know my name?

Nadine: She knows as much as she needs to know.

Brian: Does she know I have a cock? Does she know you suck it?

Nadine: (pause)

Brian: She thinks I'm a woman.

Nadine: She doesn't know.

Brian: If you didn't tell her I'm a man, she'll assume I'm a woman.

Nadine: Which is not the same as lying.

Brian: And you accuse me of being sexist.

Nadine: Heterosexist. Sometimes both.

Brian: So you're closeted.

Nadine: She was really upset. She threatened—

Brian: What? What did Catherine threaten this time?

Nadine: Something about taking Wyatt. Putting him in the car and driving.

Brian: You mean kidnapping—

Nadine: She was upset, that's all.

Brian: or driving to Whole Foods for organic baby food?

Nadine: She didn't mean what she said.

Brian: Because they're two entirely different things. (takes out a pack of cigarettes)

Nadine: Don't smoke in my house.

Brian: Candy. (offers her the pack) Want one?

Nadine: So you're selectively good at pretending.

Brian: Sugar's as real as true ash any day.

Nadine: We need to stop.

Brian: (pretends to light her cigarette)

Nadine: We need—

Brian: to stop.

Nadine: But I can't stop.

Brian: I can't either.

Nadine: Now what?

Brian: Now nothing. We do nothing, now. We keep doing what we do.

Nadine: But Catherine…

Brian: You shouldn't have told her.

Nadine: (stares)

Brian: Just saying.

Nadine: (stares)

Brian: We had a good thing, and nobody needed to know.

Nadine: Or.

Brian: Or?

Nadine: Or we could just come out.

Brian: You mean divorce.

Nadine: You could tell Brianna. And we could just come out.

Brian: Nadine, I have a life—

Nadine: You, me, and Wyatt. No more sneaking around.

Brian: You want me to tell Brianna.

Nadine: Not about Wyatt. Just about me.

Brian: Great. I'll start with you: "Hey, Brianna, I've been having an affair for two years, but don't worry, I'm not going to tell you about the baby."

Nadine: (shakes her head)

Brian: Like what, then? What Lifetime movie?

Nadine: You're Wyatt's father.

Brian: You should've thought of that in Palm Beach.

Nadine: So you're saying no.

Brian: I'm saying this is a new idea and I need to think about it.

Nadine: Which means no.

Brian: C'mere. (pulls Nadine toward him; Nadine pushes him away)

Nadine: Two years and a kid but you want to stay with Brianna?

Brian: Sweetheart. Nothing has to change.

Nadine: I can't do this anymore.

Brian: Then don't.

Nadine: (stares)

Brian: Then walk away.

Wyatt: (crying)

Nadine: Oh, honey, I'm here. (goes into the other room) Shhhh baby. Shhhh little baby. I'm here, mama's here, I got you. There, there.

Fade to black.

AFTERIMAGE

The woman whose daughter had been hit by a car rode the school bus each morning. She sat in the back, messing up alphabetical order. Pretty, like someone's mom on TV, and it was like TV when the cops showed up. She sat in homeroom with her knees all scrunched. Cops held her elbows and walked her outside.

After that, school was boring again. Wyatt counted minutes until the final bell, which carried him along on a flood of oversized backpacks. If he could get past bullies he'd be home by now, and then he was, crunching on an apple from a stranger's tree.

"Mom," he said, "that lady was in school again today."

His mother didn't answer, but he kept talking; it was his way. "Mom, that lady was at it again."

Wyatt remembered when she became part of the pack. She wore skinny jeans and sat by herself. Jason passed her a stick of gum. She blew epic bubbles and left the chewed up gum stuck under her seat. When she was a mom, she seemed scary, doing things no mom should do. They made her a kid and then she fit in. Nothing about school was interesting. None of his teachers could keep up with technology. They wrote stuff on the board in chalk. They were scared of loud noises and the sketchy kids who kept their heads down.

The dead girl's mom was different. She was the way they wished moms could be. Wyatt figured if he'd known the dead girl, they would've hung out, bike riding and stuff.

The car that hit her was a teacher's car. The teacher was texting, and then went to jail. It was the year before Wyatt got his own phone and the year before they moved downhill.

Wyatt's phone rang, a nameless number. He wasn't supposed to answer strangers.

"Hello?"

"Hi Wyatt, it's Jocelyn. Your friend from homeroom."

The dead girl's mom. But why would she call him?

There was an ease in her voice that comforted, as though it led into darkness from which one never wanted to return. Jocelyn, Jocelyn. Would he ever know a girl so well?

"Jocelyn," she repeated.

"Yes, what," Wyatt replied.

"Have you ever heard a string quartet at sunset?"

Was she asking him on a date? "You know I'm only 11, right?"

"They played at my wedding. I was thinking of that when she was born. Like 'sunrise, sunset,' you know?"

Wyatt didn't know what to say. "Why are you telling me this?"

"We were in tents because the day had threatened rain. Isn't that funny now? Threatened? I was so worried. We both were. That the rain would ruin things, the mud. That everyone would be sorry they came somehow. That our wedding wasn't enough of an event to overcome the usual daily griefs in a person's life. That rain would decide the day was bad. Or mud would. Or that we were. I didn't know then about rain being a good thing. Meaning something about fertility, about children. Maybe that it threatened was enough to give us the child. I can't say her name. Maybe that it threatened was enough to give us the child, but not enough to keep her. I think about that string quartet and I want to not have seen the sun, that light making everything orange red. The sun setting so brutally once it dropped below the tent's eaves. How we couldn't look in that direction. And how when the quartet played and the sun set and we danced and sometimes I'd be turned around in some move, twirled—she used to twirl me—that I'd get

caught in that sun. So bright it was. So bright. I remember the afterimage—that's what it's called—the afterimage floating over everything.
I wonder if that was the child. If I follow it, I name it. Afterimage.
Really that's called photo-bleaching and happens to the cells in your
retina, which is the light-sensitive part of your eye, way back in the
back, at the back of your eye. The cells there actually break down,
you know, in overexcitement, and then rebuild and that black spot,
then red spot, then yellow—you know what I'm talking about?—it's
the cells regenerating. I want to call that afterimage Cora. There and
then not there in the brightness." She trailed off then. "There and not
there. I wish it would rain."

Wyatt said nothing, but made his breath a little louder so she
would know he was there. And then she hung up.

◆

On the way to the bus stop the next morning, Wyatt made a point
to look at the sun, then look away, letting the black-red orb dart over
everything.

James and Kevin and Alex were standing in the same configura-
tion as always, James in the middle. All three turned their heads at
the same time as Wyatt approached. And Wyatt remembered the last
beating. How he'd gone home throat and arm bruised and his lower
lip cut open, the metal taste in his mouth. The boys turned their heads.
I'm going to look at the sun again, Wyatt thought, and everything will
be okay, round orb, a second head, there will be two of me. And so he
did, and so there was. And the boys magically left him alone.

Jocelyn wasn't on the bus. And she wasn't in homeroom. Wyatt
picked at every hangnail on his left hand until it bled, then the right.
Taking penance for the blood he'd not shed at someone else's hands.
His fingers were raw with an acute and delicious pain. Like the fine
point of a pencil moving perfectly across fresh paper. He could feel
his heart by the throbbing in seven of ten fingers and he knew which

ones without looking. This is what being alive means, he thought. This is what having a body is.

In biology class he stared vacantly at the board, silently accounting for all of his parts in succession. Foot, I can feel a foot. And the other one. I can feel my ankles; he rotated them. And so on, up to his lap, where he imagined his penis, the loose flesh he'd only started connecting with when the house was completely empty. And then he started over, from the top of his head, feeling the imagined burning in his scalp of his hair growing, his ears itched. He opened his eyes wide to really feel them, ran his tongue along teeth. He thought about his arms a long time. All of this, he thought. As he did every day. All of this, and I don't have to pay for a thing. Even when my lip is bleeding, or blood comes blackly to the surface in some swell, it's mine, he thought. We all just get this. And it all works, it all does things. And he thought of the girl in the road for whom nothing worked anymore. How was that possible. He thought of her hair, her own burning scalp. Her itchy ears. The blood around her mouth. What he'd heard about. How one leg bent back, and the other one bent oddly too, and the eyes wide open, bloodshot instantly. Who had told him that. He thought of the bent legs. The legs that had worked and the arms and the spot in her lap he couldn't even fathom, but had heard about.

♦

It was five months later before he would see that spot for himself in another girl. By then Jocelyn had quit coming to school altogether and though he hadn't forgotten about her, the conversation they'd had seemed far enough away to have maybe not happened at all.

Wyatt had made a truce with James earlier in the year, predicated on Wyatt helping out with homework, never once hesitating when asked, and perfecting the abbreviated hello that took the *what* out of what's up. "'Sup," Wyatt said as he entered James's house. "'Sup," James said. It was summer and Wyatt handed over a stack of papers meant to be James's final essay for Social Studies summer school. James went back to the TV where some sports was happening.

"You can get a beer if you want, Wy. But don't let Rachel see."

Rachel was James's sister, 18, at home for summer break. Wyatt knew she didn't care James drank, didn't know why he would say that.

Wyatt went into the kitchen, but thought better of it. He took out a Win-Pop instead and stood at the fridge reading the calendar tacked to the front of it, looking at pictures. Somebody's baby.

"This you?" Wyatt shouted into the other room. The sweet fizz scorched down his throat.

James didn't answer and Wyatt moved on. Baby, baby, baby, wedding invite, girl on a horse, business cards, dentist appointment card with a cartoon tooth sporting googly eyes, a coupon for ice cream, an oil change punch card. Then he moved down the hall. It was only the second time he'd been to James's house and the time before James was all over him, talking about stupid shit. The weightlifting bench in the basement his dad had gotten, the family trip they were going on to Key West, the car his dad was working on that would be his one day. Things Wyatt had no context for.

"What happened to your dad?" James had asked.

Most kids had heard some things.

"Cancer," Wyatt always said, which was tragic enough.

"He lose all his hair?"

"Yes," Wyatt said.

"Fuck," James said.

"Does anyone ever call you Jim?" Wyatt asked.

"No," James said. And the conversation was as good as changed. The onslaught of boyhood continued as they looked at the Warhammer figurines crowding the shelf above his bed. Wyatt didn't know Warhammer either.

"I'm cutting them apart and re-making them, designing and adding new weapons."

Wyatt wanted to say, this means nothing to me, but instead looked at James's hands moving over the figures, looked at his red lips rounding out words. A mouth, just like I have, thought Wyatt. Arms and legs too. How did we get them? He thought about opening James's mouth with a slap; he thought about kissing him after, the blood taste.

"… soldering together," James was saying. And then more about his father and tools.

Is this what having friends is for? To examine other bodies up close and imagine the things they can do? Wyatt thought of James's fist, which though smallish had brought out blood from Wyatt's mouth on more than one occasion. He thought of James's teeth, crooked, but not so crooked it slowed him down. And now he was in the other room doing nothing with his body, which was also his right. Feet on the coffee table, hand around a beer, head swimming probably. The way the warmth will do. Wyatt had had beer before. Drank all the beer in the fridge the weekend his dad left, went into the garage and sat down on the cement. He felt like his head was plugged in to something, warming slowly, then staying hot and spinning. He lay on the cold floor, damp from a week of rain, and watched the ceiling for movement in the cobwebs. There was none. And then he fell asleep. That's what drinking seemed to be: warmth and then sleep. It wasn't anything he needed.

The door was open at the end of the hall. He knew it was her room, Rachel's. He looked at the pictures in the hall. James at various ages. Rachel in an awkward stage. And some sepia-toned prints. People looking grim at the camera. He looked at the pictures in the dim hall, all the while keeping an eye on the open door. Maybe she wasn't home and he could go in there, see what a girl who is nearly an adult or maybe already an adult—Wyatt could never remember if 18 made you so or 19. Something about 19 made more sense, brushing right up against that next decade. Wyatt wanted to see where she put her things, how they were arranged. He wanted to look in the closet to see the clothes hanging there, limp bodies with all the life sucked out of them.

"What are you doing?" Rachel said to him. He couldn't see her.

"What?" Wyatt said.

"I can hear you out there, creeping around."

"I'm just looking at the pictures."

"Weirdo," she said.

"What?" Wyatt said.

"You're a weirdo is what I said. Why aren't you watching the game with James?"

Still he couldn't see her. The hall was dark, her room bright and it smelled nice. Or he imagined it did.

"What?" Wyatt said. More because he couldn't think of anything to say than because he hadn't heard her.

"Come here," Rachel said.

Wyatt went to the doorway. It was not what he expected. Black-and-white photographs, framed. No posters, nothing pink. There was a framed portrait of David Bowie on the nightstand. He smiled.

"What?" Rachel said.

"Ziggy Stardust," he said.

"And you're some Spider from Mars, I suppose?"

"You know he was only that for one year. Everyone wanted him to continue, but he didn't. Ziggy died and everything."

"Now I know," Rachel said.

"Know what?" Wyatt said.

"Why you're not watching the game."

"Oh," he said.

She was lying on her bed, blue-gray comforter, orange pillows. She didn't give him the reason like he thought she would. She just looked at him.

So he asked. "Why?"

"Because you're a faggot."

Wyatt stood there watching the word form in her mouth. Her top teeth on her bottom lip started the whole thing. She had one hand behind her head, one on her stomach. Her arms were similar to his, he thought, though the hands were different, fingers longer, no hangnails. He looked at her hand resting there on her stomach like some cat. So he didn't have to look back at her mouth, which was smiling now.

"I'm kidding," she said.

The hand on her stomach slid down to her waist. Wyatt looked back at the Bowie photo.

"What's your name?" she said.

"Wyatt," he said.

"I'm just kidding, Wyatt. I know your name."

"Why did you ask then?"

"I was just kidding."

"Oh."

"Wy?"

"Yes?"

"People call you Wy."

"Some people," he said.

"Why?"

"*Why?*"

She laughed then. "Does it bother you? A name that's a question?"

"No," he said.

"No, what?"

"No it doesn't bother me."

"No, what?"

"*What?*" he said.

"No, ma'am. It doesn't bother me," Rachel said in some voice that was probably supposed to be imitating him. It didn't bother him. Nothing right now could bother him, though he couldn't decide what to do with *his* hands. His pockets seemed so far away. Any movement to get his hands in there would seem dramatic. But he couldn't keep them so stiff at his sides. What does one do with hands to make them not seem alien? Are these mine? He suddenly thought. For the first time, his body seemed a little bit not his. He put one hand on the door jamb.

"What are—" Wyatt started.

"Do you want to come in?" Rachel said. "You look uncomfortable. What were you going to ask?"

"What are you doing?" he asked. He meant to ask what she was studying in school, but somehow this other thing came out of his mouth, like his mouth wasn't his anymore either.

"What am I doing? What do you mean? Like, right now?"

"I meant to ask what you've been learning about in school."

"Maybe it's the same answer," Rachel said.

"What do you mean?"

"Human sexuality," she said.

"Oh," Wyatt said.

"Oh," she said. "Oh, he says."

"Well, I should probably—" he started again.

"I don't really think you're a faggot, Wy." He could get used to a nickname if she said it. Wy.

"Okay."

"Have you ever been in love, Wy?"

Wyatt thought about Jocelyn, though he wasn't sure why.

"No," he said. "I don't think so. I should probably go back…" He ended the sentence there he knew because he did not want to bring her brother's name into the room just then.

Rachel moved her hand over her jeans. She watched him while she did this. Stared him in the face. He watched her hand, of course. And because he was watching her hand, she rubbed it up and down along the zipper and lower than the zipper a few times. The zipper was closed, but he didn't want it to be.

"Look at me," she said.

"I am," he said.

"Look at me."

He lifted his eyes from her hand to her face.

"Do you want me to?" she asked.

And he didn't know what the question was really, only knew that the answer was yes.

"Yes," he said.

She tugged the zipper until it gave, then lifted her hips to push her jeans down a little, then her panties. He could see her hair there, in a neat little line. He looked back at her face. She was staring at him. Her arm moved slowly up and down and though he couldn't tell what she was doing exactly, he knew it was something like what he did when he looked at catalogue pictures. Everything was so hidden with girls, everything so tucked away, he was thinking. Why is this? He had heard girls had more nerve endings down there than boys did. But where were they? He wanted to ask, wanted to see more, but he was already seeing so much. The room got hot suddenly, and he wanted to ask her to open her legs wider so he could see, pull down her pants all the way and open her legs wide so he could see everything in there. Instead he just stood by the door. She rubbed faster and the jeans got in the way and so she paused and pushed them down a little further—*yes*, he thought—but not far enough. Her hips thrust lightly into her hand in rhythm, a thrust for every few back and forth motions, which had gotten faster, and her breathing increased. Like some strange wind was tugging at her throat. He could feel his heart beat and his penis pressed uncomfortably against his pants. But he knew better than to put his hands anywhere near there for fear she would stop. And then she let out some small animal sound and then she did stop thrusting and her hand slowed.

"Wyatt?" she said.

"Yes," he said.

"Look at me."

And he did. Her face was pink and her eyes were wild. He thought maybe this was what love was, that maybe he was in love with her.

"Get out of here," she said. "And close the door."

Wyatt got a beer out of the fridge and sat down on the couch next to James, drank it down and got another. He drank until his head felt warm and the images on TV no longer came into focus. He watched the blurred images move around on the screen and the sounds coming from them, the commentators and the sounds of the game and the spectators' cheers, until he couldn't imagine a clear world anymore and the sun was big outside, so big it seemed to beat on the windows soundlessly.

"I have to go," he said and James said nothing and didn't turn his head, just gave him the thumbs up to show he'd heard him.

On the walk he made sure to keep to the sidewalk when there were sidewalks and the graveled side of the road when there weren't. He wasn't walking straight, he knew, but felt he made decent progress with forward motion. And all his muscles warmed, felt like they were speaking to him in a language he'd not known before. There was effort in every step, but it felt good. It felt like he was on fire.

On the main road, the shoulder narrowed and the cars got closer and he thought about the girl again, her legs bent back and he thought about the warm in his legs of the blood running through them and he thought about blood outside the body, inside the body, all the things hidden away. All the everything he wanted to know about. It felt like life was starting now, really starting. His body was his and not his at the same time, could be taken from him at any moment. Wholly or just by bits, temporarily. It's mine and it's yours, he thought. It's mine and it's yours and I give it to you for nothing.

The cars whipped by one after another. And then he turned into her driveway. It had been a long walk, but he was finally there. Jocelyn's house with its fading trim, the sun setting harshly behind it.

ACKNOWLEDGMENTS

Thanks to the publications where versions of these stories first appeared:

District Lit: "The Appeasement"
Hawai`i Pacific Review: "True Ash"
The Mondegreen: "Ash"
Not Just Another Pretty Face: "50th Anniversary of a Man-Made Lake"
Sonora Review: "A Woman With A Gun"
Zymbol: "To Keep You Close" and "Cake"

Carol and Elizabeth would like to thank their family and friends. Special thanks to Corinne Botz and all our colleagues at Black Lawrence Press.

Elizabeth J. Colen is most recently the author of *What Weaponry*, a novel in prose poems. Other books include poetry collections *Money for Sunsets* (Lambda Literary Award finalist in 2011) and *Waiting Up for the End of the World: Conspiracies*, flash fiction collection *Dear Mother Monster, Dear Daughter Mistake*, long poem / lyric essay hybrid *The Green Condition*, and fiction collaboration *Your Sick*. Nonfiction editor at Tupelo Press and freelance editor/ manuscript consultant, she teaches at Western Washington University.

Carol Guess is the author of numerous books of poetry and prose, including *Darling Endangered, Doll Studies: Forensics,* and *Tinderbox Lawn*. In 2014 she was awarded the Philolexian Award for Distinguished Literary Achievement by Columbia University. Recent BLP titles include *With Animal*, co-written with Kelly Magee, and *Human-Ghost Hybrid Project*, co-written with Daniela Olszewska. She is Professor of English at Western Washington University.